HOW
NOT
TO BE A
VAMPIRE
SLAYER

HOW NOT TO BE A VAMPIRE SLAYER

KATY BIRCHALL

SCHOLASTIC INC.

Copyright © 2023 by Katy Birchall

Interior art © 2023 by Carissa Harris

All rights reserved. Published by Scholastic Inc., *Publishers since 1920.*

SCHOLASTIC and associated logos are trademarks and/or registered trademarks of Scholastic Inc.

First published in the UK by Scholastic Children's Books, an imprint of Scholastic Ltd., Euston House, 24 Eversholt Street, London, NW1 1DB, UK

The publisher does not have any control over and does not assume any responsibility for author or third-party websites or their content.

ISBN 978-1-338-89309-0

10 9 8 7 6 5 4 3 2 1   23 24 25 26 27

Printed in the U.S.A.   40

First printing 2023

Book design by Omou Barry

For Margaret

As darkness falls, a cloaked figure, hidden in the looming shadows of the gnarled, twisted trees, sweeps silently closer to the trickling stream that runs around the edge of Skeleton Woods.

He stops at the end of the tree line to look out across the field lying ahead, at the top of which sits a lone, wonky house. As he patiently waits, a colony of bats bursts through the branches of the trees and swarms around him in a tornado of fluttering wings. He doesn't flinch. Instead, he welcomes the creatures with a sinister smile that reveals a set of sharp, gleaming white fangs.

Eventually, in the distance a car trundles up the narrow, bumpy road toward the house, coming to a stop at the gate. The car doors swing open and a man and woman climb out the front, followed by a young girl from the back. They stand at the gate together, looking up at their new home.

The family do not know they are being watched.

"They have a daughter," the cloaked figure says quietly to himself as the bats settle in the trees surrounding him. "I wasn't expecting that."

Suddenly, the girl turns to look at the woods, staring right at him. For a moment, he's startled. It's almost as if . . .

No. He shakes his head. He must be imagining it. For her human eyes to see him from across the field, especially as the sun has set and he is hidden by the trees, she'd have to be . . .

But that can't be right. Not her, a child.

Strange, though. It was as though she *knew* he was there.

It's impossible. Of course she couldn't see him. He chuckles, a low, threatening hiss that echoes through the woods. He is showing his age. He's been doing this too long. His imagination is starting to get the better of him.

"Come, my friends, we have work to do," he announces to the bats, who screech in excitable chorus. "There are new residents at Skeleton Lodge and we must begin our preparations to welcome them."

He pauses, watching the girl walk through the gate toward the house, a wicked smile creeping across his lips.

"After all, I'm sure they'll be *dying* to meet their neighbors."

With a menacing cackle, he turns on his heel, sweeping his billowing cloak around him, and disappears back into the shadow of the trees, his bloodred eyes flashing in the darkness.

W ell," Mum says, gesturing excitedly at our new house, "what do you think?"

I take in the grubby white walls, the chipped, flaking blue paint of the rickety front door, and the smeared windows that look as though they were last opened in the Stone Age.

"The house is . . ." I search for the right word, tilting my head at an angle. ". . . wonky."

"Yes, Maggie, it is," Dad chuckles, stretching after the long drive and throwing his arm around me. "I think there's something charming about living in a wonky house, though, don't you? As long as it doesn't fall over!"

Mum joins him in laughing heartily at this, but I don't get the joke. The house really does look like it might topple over. As my parents cheerily turn back to the car to start unloading some of our stuff, I stay standing at the broken

wooden gate in front of the winding, overgrown path leading up to the house.

When Mum and Dad announced out of the blue two
weeks ago that we were moving to a town I'd never heard
of called Goreway, which was in the middle of nowhere on
the Yorkshire coast, I thought they had maybe lost their
minds.

Now, looking at this run-down house, I KNOW
they have.

This house isn't even in the town. We drove through
the main street to get here and then kept on going for a
while, right past all the other clusters of houses. This one is
on the outskirts, completely on its own in the middle of a
field, which happens to border a huge woodland.

I look over my shoulder at the edge of the woods. It's
hard to make much out in the dark, but I can see the
gnarled tree trunks are thick, tall, and strangely twisted,
their branches creaking eerily in the wind.

Suddenly, I see something in the shadows behind
them—two red dots—and squint to make it out.

"Skeleton Woods!" Dad says suddenly, making me jump.
Coming to stand next to me, holding a heavy box, he nods
toward the trees, his forehead furrowed. "An ancient

woodland, full of history . . . and stories. You're not to go in there. No one is allowed."

"Why not? What kind of stories?"

"All sorts," he says, his eyes gleaming. "Some say—"

"Don't listen to your dad," Mum interrupts, shaking her head and nudging him in the ribs as she passes on her way up to the house. "The reason you're not to go in there is because it's big and people get lost. Nothing to do with ghosts and ghouls."

"Ghosts and ghouls?" I ask in amazement, staring wide-eyed at the woodland, wondering what it was that I saw lurking in there before. "Is it *haunted*?"

"See what you've done?" Mum sighs, narrowing her eyes at Dad. "She won't let it go now."

"I wasn't the one who mentioned ghosts and ghouls," Dad points out, chuckling.

Mum is right, I won't let this go. I don't know why, but I've always been wild about horror stories. When I was little and my parents read to me before bed, I would make them tell me scary stories, forcing Dad to turn off the lights and hold a flashlight beneath his chin, lighting his face up in a spooky way. I love that feeling of suspense, of being on the edge of your seat, not knowing what's going to happen next. Whenever we go to fairs or theme parks, I'm only really interested in the scary rides, the "haunted houses" where actors dressed as mummies and skeletons jump out at you from the darkness, making you scream your head off, before you burst out laughing at yourself for being so silly.

I guess you could blame my love of scary stuff on Dad. He's just as into it as I am, and Mum always rolls her eyes at us when it's our turn to pick a film for movie night. Annoyingly, they're both strict about which ones I'm allowed to watch.

"You're eleven years old," Mum reminds me when I try to persuade them to let me watch something that looks truly terrifying. "Trust me, you'll get nightmares."

That's the thing, though—I don't. I've never had night-mares. I know that's weird. Everyone has had a nightmare at least *once* in their life. But I NEVER have. Not one. I don't feel chilled to the bone after reading a horror book or watching a scary film. I'm just *fascinated* with them. My favorite thing is trying to work out how the hero is going to win before the end. How can anyone possibly defeat a ghost? How can a human destroy a league of vampires? What will they do to stop that monster? My brain is always too busy trying to answer those questions, while everyone else is screaming or hiding behind a cushion.

Weird, I know.

"Stop staring at the woods, Maggie," Mum says with a knowing smile, jolting me from my thoughts. "It's only old folktales and stupid stories."

"There are folktales about those woods, then?" I ask eagerly, getting my phone from my pocket. "I want to read about them."

Mum clears her throat pointedly. "It's going to be pitch-black soon. You can read up on it *after* you've helped us unload the car. Got it?"

Mum can be quite intimidating when she wants to be. She has this stern voice that she reserves for the times when she really means it. Once the stern voice comes out, you know to listen. I reluctantly put my phone away.

"Come on, then," Dad chuckles, jostling the box in his arms. "Let's go explore our new house!"

Feeling a lot more enthusiastic about the house now that I know the woodlands nearby have some cool history, I grab my backpack from the car and also a pillow, so it looks like I'm helping, and traipse after them, kicking through the weeds to the front door. Mum unlocks it and pushes it open enthusiastically, turning on the lights as we head into the hall.

Mum and Dad came down here last weekend along with the movers to furnish the house with the majority of our things and get it ready for moving in, so it's comforting to see some of our furniture already dotted around, but the house is very poky compared to our old place and the ceilings are so low that Dad is going to have to watch his head ducking through the wooden-beamed doorways.

But I like it. It's different.

"It needs a lot of work," Mum sighs, putting her hands on her hips as she looks about us. "But we can make this homey in no time."

"That's right," Dad says. "I'm afraid my uncle Bram clearly didn't look after the house too well when he lived here, but it has such potential! Just you wait and see, Maggie."

"It's cool," I say, noticing a large cobweb in the doorway to the kitchen.

"Why don't you go pick your room?" Mum suggests. "You get first choice!"

Still clutching my pillow, I head up the creaky stairs and take a good look at all the options. One of the rooms is a lot bigger than the others and is clearly the main bedroom—that one must have been Great-Uncle Bram's—so I leave that to Mum and Dad, and decide on the second biggest, which is on the other side of the house. Its windows look out toward the woods. All the bedrooms have gigantic, heavy-framed mirrors in them. I conclude that Dad's uncle must have been very vain.

I never met Great-Uncle Bram. I'd barely heard of him before two weeks ago when he passed away and left us this old, creepy house. When Dad told me we were moving here, I asked a lot of questions about this Uncle Bram, but Dad could barely tell me anything. They'd lost touch years ago. All he said was that Bram kept to himself, and lived a very isolated life.

Now that I'm here, I can see how that happened. There's no one for miles.

I thought it was strange that he would leave his house to us when I'd never even heard of him before, but Dad just shrugged and said it was because we were his only family and he didn't have anyone else.

I sit down on the bed and get my phone out, ready to google Skeleton Woods, but there's no signal. I try standing on the bed and holding my phone up to see if that helps, but get zero bars. I wander around the room with no luck before giving up, slumping down on the bare mattress and peering out the window. It's so *quiet* here.

Mum and Dad are now making their way back down the path to the car, and I smile as they pull out suitcases from the trunk, chatting excitedly about the plans they have to do the place up. I already feel like we're going to be much more at home here than we ever were in London.

Mum has always wanted to move to the countryside. My parents are both dentists and worked in the same practice; that's how they met all those years ago. They decided to live near their work because it made sense, but Mum has often talked about how she'd love to move out to a country village and have her own little practice there, as part of a small, friendly community.

I guess that's why they decided to move here so quickly. Great-Uncle Bram leaving them this house couldn't have been more perfect. And just as Mum dreamed it, Goreway has a small, overrun dental practice, which is in desperate need of help—apparently the dentist there has been wanting to retire for a while now, but there was no one to take over. He advertised the job last year and didn't get any applicants because no one wanted to move to such an obscure little town. Mum and Dad got jobs here straight away and have grand plans to make the practice bigger and better.

"There you are," Mum says, appearing in my doorway, pushing her hair back from her forehead. "Good choice on the room. All your boxes are in the big bedroom. Shall we move them in here and then you can start unpacking? Dad is going to put the kettle on so we can have a nice cup of tea."

"Sure," I say, jumping to my feet and following her to the stack of boxes in the main bedroom. "Mum, when do we get Wi-Fi? There's no signal here."

"Monday," she informs me, examining the scrawled black marker writing on the side of the boxes, working out which one's which.

"No internet for the whole of tonight and tomorrow?" I say, wrinkling my nose.

"I know, we'll have to talk to one another and stuff," Mum teases, handing me my first box. "I wouldn't worry. We have lots of exploring to do to keep us busy. We can go check out the town. We may even be able to go have a sneak peek of your new school," she adds brightly. "Depending on whether we have time."

I'm instantly hit by a wave of nerves.

I've never been very good at school. I always got the same thing in my reports: I was easily distracted and had to stop drifting off into daydreams. I wasn't good at the "friends" side of things, either. I wish I were one of those people who could make friends easily, the ones who always know the right thing to say to get people to like them.

Nina Delby is one of those people. She was the most popular girl in my old school, and two years ago she invited me to a sleepover, along with all the girls in our class. I wasn't exactly unpopular then, I was just quiet compared to the others, but it was nice of her to invite me when I wasn't part of her group. I think she didn't want anyone to feel left out.

Anyway, that was the night it all went wrong.

We were all in the sitting room in our pajamas, eating ice cream and listening to music, when Nina announced it was movie time. Nina's parents were nowhere near as strict as mine, and they left us alone to pick our own film.

I still don't know why I decided *that* was the time to speak up.

I could have stayed quiet. I didn't have to say anything. I could have continued eating my ice cream happily, nodding along to whatever movie someone else suggested. That's not what happened. Instead, I said we should watch this AMAZING film I'd heard about called *Vampires at Dawn*.

"Oooh," one of the girls said. "Is that the one with the vampire at school? I've heard that's really funny!"

I didn't know what she was talking about, but because I didn't really know the plot, I shrugged and said, "Maybe!" Nina said that sounded good and so she found it and pressed play. We all settled down to watch a nice film.

It was a total DISASTER. It was not about a vampire at school, and it was not funny. It was terrifying . . . for everyone else. I was the only one who enjoyed it. The others screamed their heads off the whole way through, and one girl, who happened to be Nina's best friend at the time, even started crying. Apparently they all had nightmares for weeks, and my parents got a lot of phone calls from furious parents. I was grounded for a LONG time.

Nina told me I ruined her party and, after that, barely spoke to me again. A few days later, I was walking past a group of them and overheard her say, "Maggie Helsby is a total FREAK." That reputation stayed with me for the next two years, so when Mum and Dad announced we were moving and I would be leaving my school, I was very happy about it.

But what if I mess it up again? What if all the kids at my new school don't like me, either?

What if I am just a big freak? *FOREVER?*

"It's natural to feel nervous," Mum says, reading my expression as she helps me carry boxes through to my new bedroom. "Everyone feels that way when they start a new school."

"I know." I nod, swallowing the lump in my throat. I place a box down on the floorboards and then straighten up, looking out the window across to the woodland, letting out a long, hopeful sigh. "I just really hope things are different here."

G oreway School doesn't look like a school at all.

    As we turn the corner around the village green on Monday morning and it looms into view, my jaw drops and the butterflies in my stomach start fluttering like mad, making me feel sick. It's a huge, imposing stone building with tall windows and stacked chimneys dotted all over the roof.

"It's Gothic architecture," Dad says as we park on the gravel, slotting into the line of cars on the drive. "I thought you'd be pleased about that."

"For goodness' sake," Mum sighs, rolling her eyes dramatically and undoing her seat belt. "It's Maggie's first day! Can we focus, please?"

I smile gratefully at Dad, though, as he catches my eye in the rearview mirror because, strangely, I find the Gothic vibe comforting, just like he does. I climb out of the car and glance anxiously at the clusters of friends heading into the school together.

"Come on," Mum says, putting a comforting hand on my shoulder. "Let's go to the principal's office to register."

Gripping the straps of my backpack tightly, I walk across the drive and into the school, flanked by Mum and Dad, wondering which of the students bustling around us might be in my class. It's a much smaller school than my last one, but the number of people flowing into the building still feels daunting. We're directed to the principal's office by a smiley receptionist and sit in silence outside on a row of red plastic chairs.

The heavy wooden door suddenly swings open and a girl about my age stomps out, looking annoyed. Her jet-black hair is in a messy bun on top of her head and she seems to have her own take on the school uniform, her sweater sleeves rolled up scruffily, her shirt collar up, and black tights with holes in them.

"Ari Whitman!" a strained voice cries from the office, causing the girl to grimace. "I was not finished!"

A tall woman appears in the doorway, who I take to be the principal, Miss Woods. She puts her hands on her hips and lets out a long sigh, raising her eyebrows at the girl, who now has her arms folded stubbornly, her chin jutted out in defiance.

"Sorry, Miss Woods," the girl says cheerily, seeming pleased to have an audience. "I thought your *lecture* had come to an end."

"It had not," Miss Woods confirms, narrowing her eyes at her. "Ari, it is not even nine o'clock in the morning and already you're in trouble with TWO teachers. Any chance we can make sure it's not three by the end of the day?"

"As I told you," Ari says, "none of that was my fault."

"So Mr. Kelvin stuck a note to his own back, did he? And Mrs. Potts saw your nonexistent identical twin nosing around her desk, I suppose?"

Ari grins at her. "Sounds about right. Do you really think if I'd done either of those things, I would have been stupid enough to be caught? Come on, Miss Woods, you know I'm better than that."

"Uh-huh." Miss Woods gives her a look, but her mouth quivers as though she's trying very hard not to smile. "I want you on your best behavior for the rest of the day, Ari. I mean it this time."

"You mean it every time."

"And can you PLEASE do something about your

uniform?" Miss Woods says, exasperated. "At least tuck your shirt in."

"Gotcha," Ari says, before winking at me and waltzing off.

I smile at her back as she walks away, and Miss Woods runs a hand through her hair before turning to us.

"I'm so sorry about that," she begins, chuckling and shaking our hands one by one. "Ari is one of our more . . . outgoing students. Very bright and with a mischievous streak to match. Anyway, please, do come into my office. Welcome, Maggie, and Mr. and Mrs. Helsby, to Goreway School!"

I timidly follow her, ushered through the door by my parents, and we take our places in front of Miss Woods's desk as she settles behind it, rifling through her disorganized files and loose documents.

"Ah, here we go," she says, finding my file and glancing through it before clasping her hands together and shooting me a warm smile. "I think you'll be very happy here at Goreway, Maggie. I can see that you've got some good grades, and I have no doubt you'll make lots of new friends."

I purse my lips in response and Miss Woods goes back to reading the top page of the file. She seems a lot nicer than my last principal, who used to yell a lot. Miss Woods has already smiled more than I ever saw him do, and she seems a bit more at ease. Her curly brown hair is loosely tied back, as though she hasn't put much thought into it, and she's wearing black, thick-rimmed rectangle glasses and bright, dangling, colorful earrings that wobble distractingly whenever she speaks.

"I can't see any extracurricular activities down here," Miss Woods mentions, beaming at me across the desk. "Is there anything you're particularly interested in? We have lots of fun after-school clubs."

"She's a great reader," Dad chips in when I don't say anything, too nervous to speak. "She's really into the horror genre."

"Amongst other things," Mum adds, shooting him an irritated look.

"Scary stuff, eh? Wonderful!" Miss Woods says, her expression brightening, a reaction I don't think any of us were expecting. "Mr. Frank has an excellent selection of creepy, ghostly books in the library; I'm sure he can recommend you some. You know all about Goreway's spooky history, too, I suppose?"

"I haven't been able to look it up because we have no

signal in our new house," I say, sitting up in my seat, the first time I've spoken while we've been here. "But Dad mentioned Skeleton Woods is haunted."

"Ah, but the school also has a rather mysterious tale itself," Miss Woods chuckles as Mum closes her eyes in exasperation. "You must hear about—"

Just as things are getting good, Miss Woods is interrupted by a knock on the door. The receptionist pokes her head around apologetically.

"The mayor is here for his assembly talk, Miss Woods. He's getting a little bit . . . impatient," she says, giving the principal a knowing look.

Miss Woods acknowledges her with a nod. "Tell him I'll be right there."

As the door closes again, Miss Woods pushes back her chair and stands up, prompting us to do the same.

"I'm sorry we can't chat for longer. Mayor Collyfleur has asked to give a talk for the students in today's assembly," she explains, her chirpy tone sounding a bit forced.

"How generous of him!" Mum comments. "That sounds like it will be very interesting."

"Uh . . . yes. Yes, I'm sure. Very interesting," Miss Woods says hurriedly, looking unconvinced. "Well, it is lovely to meet you, Maggie, and a huge welcome to Goreway School. I'll get someone to show you to your classroom."

Promising my parents I'll be well looked after, she ushers us out of her office and back into the waiting area. She gives Mum and Dad a quick goodbye before scurrying over to where a grumpy man with greasy, slicked-back hair, wearing a three-piece blue suit, is standing by the door, checking his watch impatiently.

An older student, following instructions from the receptionist, comes over to show me to my classroom, and I nervously wave at my parents as I'm led away, feeling like I might throw up any second. We go through a maze of corridors until we reach the right, noisy classroom.

"There you go," the older student says, gesturing at the door. "Good luck!"

He saunters off, leaving me standing in the doorway, watching the chaos unfold in front of me. Without a teacher there, everyone is messing around or chatting loudly, dotted around in their various groups. One boy is chasing another one, who apparently has stolen his notebook, and I almost get hit in the face by a ball of scrunched-up paper lobbed at the bin in the corner. I jump back as it flies past my nose.

"Sorry!"

I turn to see the culprit and recognize Ari from outside the principal's office. She grins at me and beckons me over to join her and the boy she's sitting with.

"Hey, I'm Ari," she begins, before poking the boy next to her in the arm. "And this is Miles."

Miles smiles at me, looking up from the book in his lap. They seem completely at odds with each other. Miles is neat as a pin, his fair hair carefully combed, his uniform perfectly straight.

"Hi, I'm Maggie," I squeak. I notice Ari is holding a pad of paper with amazing sketches all over it, mostly of dragons. "Did you draw those?"

She nods, holding them up for me to see. "Yeah, they're only rough."

"They're amazing!" I exclaim, admiring them.

"Don't let her head get any bigger," Miles comments with a wry smile.

"Thanks," she says to me, ignoring Miles. "I don't get it right every time, though. I just threw away a terrible attempt at drawing a wizard. Sorry, by the way, about nearly hitting you with it. Are you into drawing?"

I shake my head. "I'm really bad at art."

"So is Miles," Ari informs me. "You should have seen his painting of a pineapple last term. It was so terrible that the art teacher cried with laughter. She didn't even try to pretend. She just pointed at it and laughed, bent over double, clutching her stomach."

"That's a slight exaggeration," Miles grumbles, narrowing his eyes at her. "And anyway, I don't like art so I don't care that I'm not good at it."

"Yeah, you don't like paint or anything messy." Ari nods at him before turning her attention back to me to explain. "He's very particular. Look at the way he reads books. Don't you think that's weird?"

I glance at the book he's holding but don't notice anything out of ordinary.

"He refuses to bend the spine," Ari points out, noting my blank expression. "I don't know how anyone can read a book that way—it's barely open. You should see how mad he gets when I fold the corners to mark my page. Every birthday, he gives me a bookmark."

"I've given you one bookmark and it was for Christmas, along with a book I got you," Miles corrects her, rolling his eyes and then smiling up at me. "So you've just moved to Goreway? Do you live near the school? Ari and

I live next door to each other, about five minutes' walk from here."

"Our house is actually quite far out," I say, unable to believe my luck that people are being so nice to me. "It's right by Skeleton Woods."

Ari's eyes widen excitedly. "Cool! Not the one that that weird old dude used to live in? The white house that's about to fall over."

"Yeah, I think so. Skeleton Lodge. It was my great-uncle Bram's."

"Oh, sorry." Ari winces. "Didn't realize he was a relation. He . . . uh . . . wasn't that weird. Or old."

"It's fine, I never met him," I say, laughing as Ari looks relieved. "And judging by the state of the house and what I've heard about him, I can guess that he was a bit weird. Have you guys ever been into Skeleton Woods?"

They share a look.

"No way!" Miles says, shaking his head. "I'm never going in there."

Ari laughs, nudging him. "Miles believes all the stories about Skeleton Woods. I persuaded him to go near it once, because I wanted to see the gorge, but he backtracked before we could get close. Chicken."

"I would rather be a chicken than be eaten by a monster or vampire," Miles says, shuddering.

"What do you mean?" I ask eagerly. "Is that what's meant to be in there?"

"You don't know the stories?"

I shake my head. Ari opens her mouth, but before she can say anything, a teacher claps his hands loudly at the front of the classroom.

"All right, everyone, quiet down," he bellows. "Time for assembly. Make your way to the hall and PLEASE don't make too much noise."

Chairs scrape across the floor as everyone gets up to file out of the classroom. I fall into step with Ari and Miles.

"What were you about to say about Skeleton Woods?" I ask them, unable to take the suspense any longer.

"We'd need a lot more time to tell you all the stories," Miles says, clutching his book to his chest. "There are hundreds."

"But the main thing you need to know about Skeleton Woods," Ari begins, her eyes glinting at me, "is that once you go in, you never come out."

Mayor Collyfleur is a VERY serious person.

He doesn't smile once during Miss Woods's introduction to his talk, and at the end when she asks the school to welcome him with a big round of applause, he corrects her pronunciation of his name with a thunderous expression, as though she's given him a grave insult.

"It's Mayor *Collyfleur*," he insists, stomping to the lectern. "NOT Mayor *Cauliflower*!"

Ari erupts into infectious giggles before leaning into me to whisper, "Everyone always calls him Mayor Cauliflower. It makes him so mad."

"Hello, children," he bellows, clearing his throat and narrowing his eyes at his already-fidgeting audience. "You're VERY lucky to have me here today to talk to you. I'm VERY busy and, if I'm honest, this is a bit of a nuisance. But I am a VERY generous person. You are welcome."

He pauses and bows his head, as though he expects applause.

Nobody responds. Someone coughs at the back.

"Well then," he huffs, looking furious, "I see this school is rather lacking in gratitude!"

"I see our mayor is rather lacking in modesty," Ari whispers.

Miles snickers quietly and I stifle a laugh as best I can, but we make enough noise for Mayor Collyfleur to whip his head around in our direction, his beady eyes scanning the rows of faces accusingly.

"You should be QUIET when the mayor is talking!" he gruffly reminds his audience. "Especially when I am talking about such important things as urban development! Yes, that's what I'm here to tell you about today, children. Now, some of your teachers and parents"—he jabs his finger at people randomly—"will have voted AGAINST my excellent plan to build a luxury five-star golf course right here in Goreway. YOU KNOW WHO YOU ARE."

Ari rolls her eyes and leans toward me again. "He wanted to knock down your house, you know."

"My house?"

She nods. "You're lucky he didn't win that vote,

otherwise you'd never have moved here. My parents were some of the people who were leading the campaign against his golf course, but it was an overwhelming vote against him so they needn't have bothered. No one needed any persuading. He wants to tear down—"

"YOU THERE!"

We jump as Mayor Collyfleur stomps over in our direction, pointing at Ari over the people in the front few rows.

"You are TALKING," he says, his face reddening with anger. "Do you know how rude that is?"

Ari stands up and places a hand on her heart. "I'm so sorry, Mayor Cauliflower—"

"COLLYFLEUR!"

"I was simply chanting your slogan," Ari says innocently. "You know, the one you had painted on signs across the town." She clears her throat, a natural in the spotlight. "PROTECT OUR GOREWAY, BUILD MORE FAIRWAYS!" She sighs, fanning her eyes dramatically. "It's so catchy and moving."

Laughter ripples through the hall as Ari sits back down again, and Miles catches my eye.

"She's not one to shy away from attention," he says, "in case you hadn't already noticed."

"Very good!" Mayor Collyfleur exclaims, won over by her performance. "For any of you who don't know, a fairway is an area of a golf course. Golf courses are VERY important! Do you know what is not important? Woodland! Pointless woodland! Especially woodland that you're not allowed to go in!" He throws up his hands in exasperation. "Who cares about history and heritage? Nobody! Do you know what people do care about? Golf courses!"

He returns to the lectern and bangs his fist on it as Miss Woods grimaces behind him.

"I am here today, children, to teach you a very important lesson," he continues solemnly. "We need to tear down Skeleton Woods and its surroundings, and build my luxury golf course on that land."

"See?" Ari whispers as my jaw drops. "Told you."

Mayor Collyfleur inhales deeply. "I may have lost the votes last time, but next time, I will not lose. I will be proposing yet again that we get rid of that awful woods that brings NOTHING to Goreway and instead, we build something that will bring so much happiness to me . . . I mean . . . to us all. I think I've made my point clear."

Slamming his hands down on the lectern one last time, he returns to his seat, checking his watch and wiping his brow with his handkerchief. Just as he sits down, the middle button of his vest pops right off and the hall erupts with laughter.

"I don't know about you, but I feel like I learned a LOT from that speech," Ari says sarcastically, shooting me a mischievous grin and causing me to erupt into uncontrollable giggles.

At lunchtime, Ari and Miles invite me to sit at their table. I'm so used to being on my own at school that, at first, I'm too excited to eat anything. I just sit next to them grinning like an idiot. It's only my first day and already I have people to sit with at lunch. Not just any people, either: *cool* people. Ari might be the coolest person I've ever met.

If Nina Delby could see me now.

"What do you think of school so far, Maggie?" Miles asks, sipping his water.

"It's GREAT," I say a little overenthusiastically, caught up in this whole sitting-with-people scenario. "As in, it's fine. I like it here."

"Bet it's a lot smaller than your school in London," Ari comments, cutting up a tomato. "Goreway is tiny."

"I like that," I insist, realizing it's time I picked up my fork. "Have you always lived here?"

They both nod in unison.

"Miles's mum went to university with mine," Ari explains. "Then they ended up moving here together. I've been stuck with him my whole life."

"We were forced to be best friends," Miles adds as Ari steals a chip from his plate.

"He's obsessed with me," Ari says. "He's followed me around since the day I was born."

"She's constantly getting me in trouble."

"He's a dweeb."

I laugh, cutting up my baked potato. "It's so cool that you live right next to each other."

"I don't know, I quite like the idea of living where you are, Maggie, and not having a next-door neighbor who walks in whenever she likes, steals your food, makes everything untidy, and then expects you to help with her homework," Miles says.

"You wouldn't last one day in Skeleton Lodge," Ari snorts. "You'd be too scared."

"Can you tell me some of the stories about Skeleton Woods?" I ask.

Ari hesitates. "I don't want to freak you out. You have to live right next to it."

"I won't be freaked out, I promise," I assure her. "I like scary stories."

She raises her eyebrows. "Are you sure?"

I nod. They share a look and then Miles takes a deep breath.

"The story goes," he begins in a low voice, "that anyone who wanders into Skeleton Woods never comes out—"

"I already told her that part," Ari interrupts, bored.

"I know!" he says, turning to her crossly. "I'm just setting the scene!"

"Oh. Sorry."

"As I was saying," Miles grumbles while Ari steals another chip from his plate, "anyone who wanders into Skeleton Woods never comes out. For there, deep within the trees—"

"Ooh! Tell her about the castle!" Ari says, grabbing his arm.

"I was just getting to that bit!"

"Cool." She nods as I giggle at Miles's furious expression. "Continue."

"Now I know how Mayor Cauliflower felt this morning," Miles sighs. He leans back in his seat, giving up. "Basically, Maggie, there's a creepy castle in the woodland

and lots of monsters, vampires, and ghosts who will steal your soul and turn you into one of them."

"There's not *really* a castle in that woodland, though," I reason, but they both nod vigorously at me.

"Look it up if you want," Ari says, taking a sip of water. "A ruined, ancient castle with spirits that still roam its halls. In the past, people have gone into Skeleton Woods to try to find the castle, but they've never lived to tell the tale. Historians, explorers, ghost hunters, all sorts. Then, like a few hundred years ago or whatever, the town decided to rule that no one should ever go in there again, and that rule has been obeyed ever since. You can't even go walk a dog in those woods. It's all out-of-bounds."

"We get some tourists who come and take photos of the outside of it, you know, people who are into the paranormal. It's quite famous in those circles," Miles notes. "Your great-uncle Bram hated people like that. He used to chase them away, saying they were tempting a terrible fate. Mayor Cauliflower really didn't like him because he drove away all the tourism we had."

"So, no one is allowed in the woods?" I ask, enraptured.

"There's no law against it or anything, but nobody goes in. No adults, no one. We grew up hearing the stories, and it's like the one rule everybody in Goreway knows. You don't go into Skeleton Woods."

"If that's the case, then why didn't the town let Mayor Cauliflower tear it down and build a golf course?" I ask curiously. "I'm obviously glad you didn't, but it's not like you're using the woods."

"Are you kidding? Skeleton Woods is the ONE claim to fame that Goreway has!" Ari says, Miles nodding in agreement. "This town is boring and tiny. Nothing ever happens here. But we do have Skeleton Woods and all the creepy stories about it. It gives Goreway an edge."

"It's part of our heritage," Miles confirms. "And anyway, if Mayor Cauliflower got his way, he'd tear down the whole town to build a giant golf course just for him. He's the worst."

"Poor Miss Woods having to let him give a talk this morning. There's no chance she asked him; he would have *told* her he was giving a talk today."

I stab my potato with my fork a few times, deep in thought.

"We haven't freaked you out, have we?" Ari asks, watching me closely. "You're not going to have nightmares or something, and then refuse to live in that house, right? My mum will kill me if she finds out I told you all this."

"No, definitely not. I don't get nightmares," I tell them matter-of-factly, before checking myself. "I mean, I *won't* get nightmares. I just can't believe no one has been in the woods for that long. I wonder what's in there."

Ari and Miles share a look, and I worry that we're getting closer to a Nina Delby sleepover situation, so I quickly change the conversation before I can be labeled a freak.

"Tell me about the teachers we have this afternoon. What are they like? Anyone I should be worried about?"

Ari's face lights up at the excuse to launch into a funny story about the PE teacher and the time he had to shoo a goose from the swimming pool and ended up falling in. I listen avidly, a warm feeling in my stomach at how nice they're being to me, but in the back of my mind I'm impatient to get to the end of the day so I can get back to my strange new house, which, I hope, will now have Wi-Fi installed.

If I'm going to be living next to a haunted woodland, I want to know ALL the stories.

THE TERRIFYING TALES ABOUT SKELETON CASTLE

Article by Timothy Herald

Deep in the heart of Skeleton Woods in Goreway, Yorkshire, supposedly lies an abandoned castle. Surrounded by myths and legends, the original story goes that once upon a time, a cruel count from overseas was banished and trapped there after his failed attempt to overthrow the King of England, seize power for himself, and unleash a reign of terror. Betrayed by his men and his plans thwarted, he was sent to live out the rest of his days alone, locked in the dungeon of a castle deep in the woods. Over the years, the castle fell into ruin and its guards abandoned it, leaving their prisoner for dead.

But was he?

The count's body was never found and the castle has never had an owner since. Why? Because anyone who attempts to live there meets an untimely end. Writings from centuries ago reveal that Goreway locals believed that he sold his soul to have the power to take revenge on his enemies, that he roamed the woodland with his army of beasts, vampires, and the undead. That anyone who dared to seek the castle never returned.

Skeleton Woods and Skeleton Castle remain to this day out-of-bounds, an unwritten rule protected by the proud inhabitants of Goreway.

To buy one of the many books about the mysterious folktales of Skeleton Castle, _click this link here_.

"You survived your first week of school," Mum says, lifting her glass of juice. "Cheers!"

I raise my glass and clink it with hers and Dad's, before taking a slice of pizza from the box and sliding it onto my plate. Dad has been at the dental practice all day, sorting through paperwork and going over plans to get it back up and running, while Mum and I have had a nice day at home together. We drove the few minutes it takes to get to the coast and walked down the beach, even though it's cold and windy today. Goreway Beach is very strange. It's really beautiful and dramatic, but kind of eerie and empty at the same time. There are no shops there or restaurants or anything, nothing to attract any tourists.

To celebrate being here for a week, Mum announced we'd order takeout, which turned out to be an eye-opening experience. There were only two options, the Italian restaurant or the fish and chips van, both on the main street. We went with Italian, and when Mum phoned them up to order, she said the man who answered groaned loudly when she gave our address. Apparently, the owner does all the deliveries himself on his bike and our house was "much farther out than he's used to." He arrived at our door red-faced and wheezing from the exercise, and had to come in for a chilled glass of water before tackling the journey home.

The pizza is lukewarm but delicious.

"Tell us more about your *friends*," Dad says enthusiastically, taking a large bite out of his slice.

"Dad!" I frown at him, my cheeks growing hotter than the pizza.

"What?" Mum laughs. "We want to know more about

them! Miles and Ari, right? You've been talking about them all week."

"No, I haven't!"

"OK, OK," Dad says, chewing his mouthful and winking at Mum. "You haven't."

I focus on my food, trying to ignore my parents beaming so obviously at each other. Their excitement is SO EMBARRASSING. I think they were worried about such a big move, so they're being really over the top whenever something good happens here.

I like Goreway School so far, even though I feel a bit overwhelmed with all the new teachers and homework and trying to remember which classroom is which. The school is a maze and I've managed to get lost at least once a day. On Wednesday, I was looking for the science lab and accidentally disturbed the school orchestra session when I wandered into the music room and tripped over a bassoon. Ari found that story HILARIOUS.

Everyone has been really nice to me, and although it's hard to be the new girl, it's better than being the biggest freak in the school. I've made friends with some other classmates, too, but I seem to have naturally fallen into hanging out with Ari and Miles. On the second day, I was walking into school, waving bye to Mum and Dad, when Ari yelled out my name and came running up to fall into step with me, eager to show me a cool new drawing she'd done. She wanted to know if I thought she should give the dragon bigger fangs.

"Definitely," I replied without hesitation. "Bigger fangs are always better."

"Got it," she laughed, adding, "You can tell your parents are dentists!"

Miles and I get along really well, too, and he's told me about lots of books I HAVE to read. In turn, I gave him a list of scary books to try. He's starting with the Goosebumps series this weekend.

When I head up to bed after eating too much pizza, I get into my pajamas, brush my teeth, and then climb under my duvet, sitting up to look out the window at the woods as I've done every night this week. I can only see the silhouette of the trees in the darkness, and if I open my window a crack, I can hear the owls hooting among them. It's so creepy and cool.

Every night, I scan the woods for those two red dots I saw on our very first night at Skeleton Lodge. But I haven't seen them since.

"Maggie?" Dad comes into my room to say good night

and catches me staring out the window. "What are you looking at?"

"I've been reading about Skeleton Woods," I say, slumping back against the pillows as he comes to perch on the edge of my bed. "There are so many stories about it. But my favorite one is about the evil count with his army of vampires and monsters. That's the most popular one."

"You've been reading about it, huh," Dad says, tilting his head at me.

I nod. "Do you know what happened today?"

"What?"

"I was outside, walking down the path of the house, and I got all annoyed at the long, weedy grass that kept tripping me up. So, I bent down and pulled it up, and do you know what it was? *Garlic!* I pulled up all these garlic bulbs!"

Dad doesn't look very surprised. Mum must have told him my discovery.

"Your uncle Bram has planted loads and loads of garlic around the house. Don't you think that's weird?" I ask.

"It's nice to be able to grow your own vegetables," he replies, looking out the window. "We're lucky to have the chance to do that. We should grow some more. Carrots, potatoes, beans. What do you think?"

41

"Dad, there is nothing but garlic planted everywhere, and I mean it is EVERYWHERE. There must be hundreds of bulbs in the soil!"

"Garlic soup is delicious," he says calmly.

"Maybe Great-Uncle Bram believed the stories. About the evil count vampire roaming the woods," I suggest.

Dad sighs, turning to smile at me. "I think Uncle Bram was simply very much into growing his own fresh produce. Garlic is good for lowering cholesterol."

"Yeah, but that's not as interesting."

He laughs, standing up and pulling the curtains closed.

"Want me to turn off the light?" he asks as he gets to the door.

"Yes, please," I reply, switching on the lamp on my bedside table and reaching for my phone.

"Don't stay up too late reading about Skeleton Castle," he says sternly, closing the door behind him. "You'll get nightmares."

On Monday, the most amazing thing happens. Ari invites me to a sleepover.

"OK, so here's the plan," she says that morning, distracting me from my history textbook. "We're going to put a tent up in the backyard and sleep out there. It's going to be so COOL."

"What?" I ask, confused. "What tent?"

"This weekend! You can come stay over. Don't worry about bringing a sleeping bag, we have loads from when Dad tried to persuade us that a camping trip would be a good idea. It was awful. Rained the whole time. We played cards all day and I didn't win ONCE. My brothers are such cheats. And don't get me started on Mum."

"You're . . . you're inviting me to your house?" I ask, checking I've heard her right.

"Yeah. You can ask your parents and let me know. I tried to tell Miles he could put a tent up in his yard, too, but he's being boring and says he doesn't like sleeping outdoors. He's very scared of bugs. I think he's traumatized from the time I put some worms in his hair and didn't tell him for ages. They kind of fell out later and gave him a mild heart attack. Anyway, he can head back home when we go to bed. Want to come?"

"YES!" I say much too eagerly, before checking myself. "I mean, yeah, OK, cool."

I'm so excited that I can't stop talking about it the whole week. We decide that we'll toast marshmallows and then tell ghost stories, which isn't even my idea, it's Ari's. That

43

means I don't have to worry about being the weird one, because it wasn't even my suggestion! Apparently, it's a rule that when you toast marshmallows you also have to see who can scare one another the most.

"I thought you were supposed to sing songs around a campfire," Miles grumbles when Ari declares her rule as we gather at his locker.

"Nope, it's telling one another ghost stories. It's a famous tradition."

Miles looks unconvinced, but he doesn't have time to argue because he's late for soccer practice, grabbing his bag and hurrying off. Ari rolls her eyes and grins at me.

"I don't know why he's so worried. He's not the one who has to sleep outside," she points out before we walk down the corridor together to the exit. "Dad says he'll leave the back door unlocked in case we want to come in because we get too scared out in the yard. But I told him that you seem a lot braver than Miles. He was reading one of those books from your list the other day and jumped a couple of feet in the air when I grabbed his shoulder."

"They are creepy," I say, feeling guilty. "I hope he enjoys them, too, though."

"I think it's cool that you like scary stories."

"Really?" I ask, blinking at her. "It's a bit weird."

"No, it's not. Or if it is, then I'm weird for liking fantasy." She shrugs. "Did you ask your dad about the garlic all around your house?"

"Yeah." I smile at her. "He said Great-Uncle Bram must have liked garlic soup."

"He must have LOVED garlic soup," she laughs before her face lights up with an idea. "Let's tell Miles that it's because Bram once *saw* a vampire. It will seriously freak him out."

"I don't know," I say, shaking my head and pushing open the door. "There's no way he'd fall for that."

"A v-vampire?" Miles's eyes widen in horror and he pulls the blanket around him tighter. "A *real* vampire? Are you sure?"

"It's all there in Great-Uncle Bram's diaries," I say in a low, solemn voice, my face lit by Ari's phone flashlight. "Late one night, he heard a rustle in the distance. He looked across to the woods and there he saw a cloaked figure emerging from the trees. His face was pale as snow. His eyes bloodred. His sharp fangs glinting in the moonlight. A *vampire*."

Miles gulps so loudly that Ari has to stifle her laughter by stuffing her sleeping bag in her mouth.

"Great-Uncle Bram grabbed a wooden stake and—"

"He had a wooden stake lying around?" Miles interrupts.

"Yes," Ari jumps in. "And you have one hanging by your door now, don't you, Maggie? Left from when Bram lived there."

"That's right." I nod. "We do."

Miles shudders. "What happened after he grabbed the wooden stake?"

"He went outside and tiptoed toward the woods, looking all around him. He could hardly see a thing in the darkness. But Great-Uncle Bram could hear something. A soft voice in the distance."

"W-what was the voice saying?" Miles whispers.

"Uh . . . *Time for dinner. Time for dinner.*"

Ari looks unimpressed. I realize it's not my best work, but I can't think of anything else on the spot. Miles is buying it, though. He's hugging his knees to his chest now.

"Great-Uncle Bram kept going toward the woods. One step at a time. And as he got closer, the voice got louder. And louder. And louder. Then it fell silent. He raised his stake high above his head and then . . ."

Right on cue, Ari turns off her phone light and the tent plunges into darkness.

"AHHHHHHHHHHHHHHHHHH!"

Miles screeches before Ari turns the flashlight back on, both of us rolling around with laughter at his reaction.

"That was MEAN!" he cries, furious at us.

"Sorry, Miles," Ari says through hysterical giggles. "But it was too EASY."

"So you made all that up?" he demands to know. "Your great-uncle never saw a vampire?"

"No, sorry," I say, turning on my phone light, too, so the tent is much brighter.

"You are both VERY MEAN," he yells, jabbing his finger from Ari to me. "No more ghost stories."

"OK, OK," Ari says, holding up her hands. "No more ghost stories. It was fun, though, wasn't it?"

"For you two," he mutters. "You were both in on it. I can't believe that was all made-up!"

"You never know, some of it might be true," I say, shrugging. "Maybe Great-Uncle Bram did see vampires, but he never told anyone because he had no one to tell."

"Doesn't it scare you living there?" Miles asks. "All those stories about Skeleton Woods . . ."

"I find them interesting." I pause before admitting the truth. "The stories make me want to go in there and see what's true. I'd love to see the castle that inspired all of them."

"What?" Miles's jaw drops open. "WHO would want to go into Skeleton Woods willingly?"

"I would!" Ari claims, putting her hand up. "But you wouldn't come with me, Miles."

"Because it's not allowed," he grumbles. "And I want to live long enough to see my twelfth birthday."

"How does anyone know if the stories are true if no one's been in there?" I ask thoughtfully. "Aren't you guys curious?"

"Yes," Ari says at the exact same time that Miles says, "No."

Ari suddenly sits up straight, her eyes lit up with excitement, and then turns slowly to face Miles. He takes one look at her expression and shakes his head frantically.

"No, Ari. No, no, no, no, no, no!"

"Miles—"

"Ari, I have told you a hundred times," he says firmly. "I am NEVER going into Skeleton Woods. EVER. Especially not after that vampire story you just told me. We'd get in trouble if anyone found out. It's against the rules."

"Come on, Miles," Ari whines. "It will be so FUN.

Everyone at school will be so impressed that we dared to do it. We'll be famous."

"This is genuinely the start of a horror movie," Miles says, his voice high-pitched. "A group of friends go into a scary woods, and then guess who's the one who gets eaten? Me."

"No one's going to eat you," Ari says as seriously as possible, the corners of her mouth twitching as she tries her best not to laugh in his face. "Right, Maggie?"

"Right."

"And we'll go in the daytime, so it's light," Ari says.

"Why don't you two go without me?" he suggests.

"Because we need to stick together!" she insists. "And you'll just feel left out. I know you, Miles. You act as though you're not interested, but secretly you want to know as badly as we do. You don't ACTUALLY believe in vampires, do you?"

He doesn't say anything, pursing his lips together so tightly they disappear.

"And it's not like you'll be alone," she continues, reaching over and squeezing his arm. "You'll be with me and Maggie. You'll be amongst friends. We'll protect you."

He glances from her to me and back again, before lifting

his eyes to the roof of the tent and letting out a long sigh. "I'll THINK about it."

Ari sits back triumphantly. I can't stop smiling, but not because Miles said he might be willing to step into Skeleton Woods.

Because Ari said we were friends.

5

Going into Skeleton Woods is a VERY big deal.

That's what Ari and Miles keep saying. I don't see it the same way. It looks like a normal woodland to me. I guess they've heard so many stories about it growing up that it's become this big thing in their heads, but I'm not sure it's going to be THAT exciting.

I just hope we find the castle. I love the idea of these creepy, ancient castle ruins in there. How can one building create so many stories? It must be SUPER scary, otherwise nobody would believe any of the folktales. According to one legend, you can still see the marks on the wall where the evil count was chained.

We decide to go two weeks after the sleepover at Ari's. We wanted to go the first weekend after, but Miles was visiting his grandparents, so we had to wait.

It's a strange feeling not dreading going to school every

day. I used to try to hide all the time, keep my head down, try not to get anyone's attention, wait for the last bell to ring. But Goreway is different. No one thinks I'm strange, and I don't mind so much that I'm terrible at sports and not the top of the class. I have Ari and Miles. Ari gets in trouble at school all the time for talking back to teachers or being messy, while Miles gets the best grades and is brilliant at sports. The teachers love him. I don't know WHY he and Ari want to hang out with me, but I'm not complaining. We're all so different, but we just click.

I've never been part of a group before.

On the Saturday morning that we're going on our adventure, I wait anxiously at my bedroom window, pretending to be reading but glancing out the window every few seconds to see if I can spot them coming down the road.

When their bikes come into view, I jump up and run down the stairs, announcing to Mum and Dad that they're here.

"I'll get the cookies out of the oven," Dad says, clapping his hands together.

"I'll get the juice out of the fridge!" Mum replies, rushing into the kitchen.

"OK, please play it cool," I groan as they hurry around.

"I am ALWAYS cool," Dad claims, brushing cookie crumbs off his floral apron and whipping on the oven mitts.

I roll my eyes, but smile at them because they're being so nice and I feel guilty that I'm about to lie to them big-time.

I head out the front door as Ari and Miles arrive. Ari jumps off her bike, but Miles has a bit more trouble getting off his because of the gigantic backpack he's carrying, which has a hockey stick poking out the top.

"What's in there?" I ask as he takes off his helmet and pushes away the hair plastered to his forehead. "You're not even staying the night. Why have you brought sports stuff?"

"Ghostbuster here decided that he needed to be ready for any scenario," Ari says, shaking her head at him. "That's why we're late. He had to pack up the entire house."

"You won't be making fun of me when we're face-to-face with a monster and I'm able to scare him away," Miles retorts, shrugging the bag off his shoulders and letting it drop. It clangs loudly as it hits the grass.

"Yeah, because monsters are notoriously scared of hockey sticks," Ari says dryly.

"You're laughing now, but you won't be later," he warns as Ari and I share a smile. "I'm not going in those woods unprepared. Either of you bring a map?"

"Calm down, Grandpa, we have maps on our phones," Ari reminds him.

"There's no signal here, Einstein," he says smugly. "Good luck trying to find your way out with a nonworking phone."

After they've finished bickering, they both admire how wonky the house is and follow me in to say hi to my parents. Mum and Dad offer them cookies and we spend a few minutes chatting politely around the kitchen table.

"We're off now," I say, excited to get going.

"Bike ride?" Mum asks cheerily, and we nod. "Great! Have fun. Stay safe."

"I *hope* we will," Miles mutters before Ari kicks him in the shin under the table.

"Back soon!" I call over my shoulder as the three of us head out, putting our helmets on.

"I can't believe we're really doing this," Ari whispers excitedly, grabbing my arm as we get to our bikes. "What if we find the castle?"

"Then we take lots of pictures to prove we were there

and get out as fast as possible," Miles answers, wheezing as he pulls his backpack on, trying not to topple over.

We do exactly as we planned, Ari leading the way back down the path from my house so it looks like we're going toward the town, but then turning around out of sight from any of the windows and coming back via a different path behind a hedge. We keep going until we reach an old painted sign nailed into the path.

SKELETON WOODS
KEEP OUT

Ari brakes and puts one foot on the ground, looking over her shoulder at us.

"Do you think your great-uncle Bram put this sign here?" she asks, slightly out of breath.

"Maybe," I say, admiring the creepy way the paint has dried with the letters dripping. "It sounds like he didn't like anyone coming near here. He probably wanted the woods all to himself."

"Or he didn't want people to be killed by zombies."

"Zombies don't live in woodlands, Miles," Ari says. "They live in graveyards. Duh."

"Let's keep going," I say, getting a strange feeling in my stomach as I look down the path toward the woods.

It's like I'm *drawn* to the trees. Weird.

We cycle on until we reach another sign just before the line of trees at the front of the woods and a small, trickling stream running alongside them.

SKELETON WOODS
HIGHLY DANGEROUS
TURN BACK NOW

"The local council definitely didn't put these signs up," Ari comments, getting off her bike and undoing her helmet. "It looks like someone has painted them as a joke."

"Maybe they have," I say, leaving my bike lying next to hers on the grass.

"Am I the only one who has a bad feeling about this?" Miles asks, reluctantly placing his bike with ours.

"It's only because you've never been this close before," Ari assures him, going over to clap him on the back. "Well done! Last time you were much farther back before you ran off screaming."

"I did NOT scream."

"Don't forget to take your helmet off," she reminds him as we begin to walk forward.

"I'm keeping my helmet on, thank you very much," Miles replies, tightening the strap under his chin. "If a werewolf tries to bite my head, I'll have a better chance of survival."

"How many made-up creatures do you think are in here?" Ari asks, laughing.

As we get closer to the front of the woods, she stops chuckling and we all fall into silence. I glance at her face and I can see she's not as confident as she was, her forehead creased, her eyes darting at every sound. By the time we're just a few feet away, she looks as tense as Miles.

"Remember, it's only a woodland," I say cheerily as we get to the remnants of an old path leading through the trees. "Everything else is just in your head. Stories and old folktales."

"Are you sure we should be doing this?" Miles squeaks, stopping.

"I think so," Ari says, looking to me for help. "Should we?"

"Come on." I smile, nodding toward the path. "I'll go first."

As twigs and leaves crunch beneath our feet in the silence, we take our first few steps into Skeleton Woods.

The canopy of branches above us is so dense that the sunlight is blocked out almost immediately, with just a few rays breaking through. I walk on, enjoying that eerie quiet that only woods and forests can create, with the creaking and the odd hoot of a bird. I admire the way the tree trunks are so twisted, remembering reading about that in one of the Skeleton Woods articles.

"It's so *dark* in here," I whisper.

After a few more steps, I realize there's a strange mist settling. I stop, smiling to myself at how perfect a setting it is for a spooky story. It's weird, but I feel suddenly . . . comforted by it. I don't know how that's possible, but the mist is making me feel confident.

In the distance, I can hear a trickling sound, but it's not coming from the stream behind us. It's coming from up ahead.

"Didn't you mention a wooded gorge or something, Ari?" I say, my voice breaking the silence.

Ari doesn't reply. I turn around to see her and Miles standing frozen to the spot some feet behind me. I hadn't realized they'd stopped.

"Are you OK?" I ask before coming back toward them. "It's just mist. Nothing to be afraid of."

"I don't feel . . . right," Ari says, her voice wobbling. "I'm going back."

"What? Why don't you feel right?"

I try to read her expression, but she won't look at me. She's staring straight ahead, like she's in some kind of trance.

"I'm going back," she repeats, in exactly the same tone as before.

"Me too," Miles says, his eyes wide as saucers. "I'm going back."

Without another word and before I can stop them, they both spin around at the same time and run as fast as they can back through the trees to the opening.

"Wait! WAIT!" I call after them, watching them disappear. "We only just got here!"

I throw my hands up in the air and then look around me to check if there's anything that could have spooked them. But there's nothing there, just the trees and some mist. I exhale and think for a moment, wondering if I should give up and follow them out. It won't be as fun finding anything on my own, and it's not like I'm trying to prove anything by being here.

And yet . . .

It's strange, but it's like I'm being pulled to go farther

into the woods. I feel like I should keep going.

I reach into my pocket and check my phone. I have full signal! How is that possible? I decide to give Ari a call and try to persuade her to come back. If she says no, then I'll leave it and try to persuade them to come here another day. The castle won't be going anywhere. I can search for it with them another time. Maybe I can even persuade Dad to come with me. I bet he secretly wants to find the castle, too.

But before I can call Ari, I hear something. It's a fluttering sound. Like wings flapping, but lots and lots of them.

I don't even think about what I'm doing. I start walking deeper into the woods, toward the sound. I make my way through the maze of tree trunks and, as the sound gets closer, I walk faster and faster, until I'm practically running. My heart is thudding against my chest so hard, I can hear a ringing in my ears, but the whole time I feel as though I'm doing the right thing. I need to know what that noise is.

Holding up my arm in front of my face to push through a barrier of branches in my way, I emerge into a clearing. Suddenly, dozens of bats swoop down from the sky in a chaotic swarm, fluttering and flapping around me.

I yelp, ducking to the ground and covering my head with my arms until they fly away. When it's safe, I lift my head up and slowly straighten to see where they've gone.

I watch the bats fly up and soar around the jagged tower of a vast, ruined castle.

6

I found it. *I found it!*

I hop up and down on the spot, launching into a solitary celebratory dance. YES! I DID IT! I can't believe I found it! The famous Skeleton Castle, right here in front of me. And it's as cool and scary as I imagined it would be.

"And not one monster, vampire, or werewolf in sight," I declare triumphantly to no one.

Steeling myself, I walk boldly toward it. My phone starts vibrating in my pocket and I jump at the disturbance, quickly fumbling for it. It's Ari. I let it ring out before typing a quick message saying I'm fine. I don't mention the castle because I want to see her face when I tell her that I found it. I then turn my phone on silent and shove it back in my pocket.

The front door is old, heavy wood, studded with nails and dotted with chinks and holes. I peer through one, anxious to see what's behind it before I go barging in, but all I see is darkness. Using both hands, I turn the large wrought-iron doorknob until I hear the satisfactory clank of a bolt being pulled back and the door opens with a shuddering creak. I quietly tiptoe into the cold, drafty hall.

"This. Is. Awesome," I whisper, gazing around me.

I'm just about to get my phone out again to take some photos when I notice something that makes the hairs on the back of my neck stand up. The black iron chandelier hanging by chains from the ceiling is one of those really old ones made up of candles. And the candles are lit.

Someone is here.

I stay frozen to the spot, listening out for any movement, but it's eerily silent. I glance up again at the flickering candle flames to make sure I'm not seeing things before creeping forward across the hall, hardly daring to breathe. Ignoring the winding staircase to my left, I head through the huge stone archway leading to a corridor straight ahead. The first door I come to on the right is slightly ajar.

I give it a faint rap with my knuckles and, when no one answers, I carefully push it open and slip inside.

"What the . . ."

At first glance, it looks like I've wandered into an

old-fashioned study. There's a dark red armchair at an antique oak desk, which has piles of old parchment strewn across it along with an inkpot and what looks like a quill pen.

For a moment, I consider the possibility that I've stepped through a time portal and gone back a couple of centuries, but then shake the idea out of my head. It's much more likely that whoever is hiding away here likes antique things. I guess it matches the decor of the castle.

Behind the desk is a purple velvet curtain with gold tassels. Curious as to why anyone would have a curtain in their office, I walk over and pull it back before letting out a loud gasp.

Right in front of me is a long, open coffin.

"Thank goodness it's empty," I say out loud, gulping.

OK, things are officially CREEPY. I need to leave.

"Hey!" a voice behind me says. "What are you DOING in here?"

I yelp and spin around so quickly that I trip over my feet, stumbling backward and tumbling into the coffin. I try to get out, but I fell at an awkward angle and my bum is wedged in, my legs flailing around above my head as I attempt to push myself up. A hand appears to help me out and I take it, inhaling sharply at how icy cold it is to touch.

My helper's grip is strong as steel and I'm lifted out from the coffin as though I weigh nothing at all, steadying myself as I land.

"Y-you're a human!"

I look up to see a girl staring at me, aghast. She's about my age with long silver hair, bold eyebrows, a very angular face, and a strong jaw. She's wearing all black, including a cloak with an impressive collar that goes right up to her high cheekbones.

Two sharp white teeth protrude over her top lip. Her eyes are bloodred.

And a large-eared bat is sitting on her shoulder.

"Y-you're a . . . *vampire*," I croak in reply, barely able to breathe.

"I've never met a human before," she says before hesitating. "Well, one that's alive, I mean."

I take a step backward, bumping into the coffin. I'm cornered.

"How did you get in here?" she asks, clearly one to play with her food and apparently in no rush to drain the blood from my veins. "You're not supposed to get through the woods, let alone to the castle. You're not a witch, are you? I thought they'd all moved away from the area."

I don't say anything, my mouth dry, my heartbeat quickening. I desperately try to think how I can escape. I wonder if I can dodge around her somehow, but there's no way I'd outrun her. Seeing as I've already experienced her strength and she's dressed in the right outfit, I'm guessing the other rumors about vampires are true, too. That means she's going to be quick and smart.

I need to cause a distraction.

But before I can think of anything, a loud voice echoes through the castle and I hear booming footsteps getting closer and closer.

The voice startles the vampire and she turns to me with a frantic expression. Her bat swoops to the door to push it shut with his little feet.

"Quick!" she encourages me, pointing to the coffin.

"No! Wait!" I cry, holding up my arm to shield my face as she comes toward me, ready to plead for my life.

"You have to hide!" she insists in a hushed voice, grabbing my arm and practically lifting me off my feet. "And stop yelling! Get in the coffin."

I try to bat her away, but she overpowers me without much trouble. Pinning me down, she looms over me crossly.

"I'm trying to save you," she says, lifting a finger to her

lips. "Be quiet and stay in here until I tell you it's safe to come out. Unless you *do* want to be eaten by a vampire?"

I stop fighting back and shake my head.

"That's what I thought," she sighs. "Lie still, don't say a word."

With that, she disappears from view and the curtain is drawn back, shielding me from the rest of the room. I hear the door swing open and bang against the wall. I clasp a hand over my mouth, my whole body tensed in fear.

"SHARPTOOTH!" the voice rages. It's a man and he does *not* sound happy. "There you are!"

"Hey, Count Bloodthirst," she replies breezily. "What's up?"

"What's up? *WHAT'S UP?* You just completely disrupted my cloak-swishing class and then you strolled out of the classroom without any excuse, before I'm told that someone saw you sneaking into my office! And here you are! Explain yourself at once."

"I would love to. Shall we go to another room and I can explain myself there?"

"No, you can explain yourself right now."

"Really? Here? How about we go to *my* room and talk there."

"WHY would we go to your room? Firstly, I know you're buying time trying to come up with an excuse, and secondly, your room is a mess."

"That's Bat-Ears's fault. He likes to make forts out of my cloaks."

"Not this again!" Count Bloodthirst's voice thunders. "You can't blame everything on your bat! Yesterday, you said it was Bat-Ears who broke the banister and yet you were seen sliding down it moments before."

"I don't know what you're talking about," she replies innocently. "But shall we go for a nice long walk and you can explain it all to me in detail?"

"Don't you go off the subject, Sharptooth! I want you to tell me why you felt the need to disrupt my class."

"I didn't mean to—look, I tripped while swishing my cloak, and I accidentally bumped into Fangly, who was swishing next to me, and then he bumped into Nightmare, who was swishing next to him, who then bumped into Maggothead, who was swishing next to her, who bumped into Dreadclaw, and so on, until there was a big vampire domino effect."

"I see," Count Bloodthirst says tiredly. "And why are you in my office without permission?"

"I wanted to . . . uh . . . clean it for you."

"Excuse me?"

"I wanted to make up for my clumsiness in class by cleaning your office as a special surprise. But the surprise is all ruined now."

"You wanted to clean my office?"

"Don't you think it needs a clean?"

"Well, I . . . I suppose it would be quite useful."

"You see? You leave it to me and I'll have it spick-and-span in no time."

"Oh. All right. Thank you."

I hear footsteps heading away from me toward the door and I hope that he's going to take the hint to leave. I'm terrified that no matter how silent I am, he may be able to hear even the sound of my breathing.

"Sharptooth," he says, obviously pausing at the door, "you're a good student with lots of potential. The most potential out of everyone." He sighs. "You know what you're destined for. You must always remember that."

"Of course, Count Bloodthirst. How could I forget?"

Sharptooth sounds sad. Whatever he's reminded her of, she didn't want to hear it.

"Anyway, you better go finish your class and leave

your office to me! I'll let you know when it's ready."

"Very well," Count Bloodthirst says, his voice growing distant. "And don't let your bat dip his toes in my inkpot and then trample over my parchment like last time!"

"I promise!"

The door slams shut and the room falls into silence. Suddenly, her face appears above me.

"You're safe!" she declares, holding out her hand. "That was a close one."

Trembling, I let her help me out of the coffin, my knees buckling slightly as I try to stand.

"Here, take a seat," she says, guiding me to the armchair. "You must be in shock, I reckon. But you're going to need to snap out of it because we have to sneak you out of the castle. That's not going to be easy when there are hundreds of vampires milling about."

"Hundreds of vampires?" I whisper. I grip the sides of the chair, feeling very dizzy.

"How annoying that I have to clean his office now. Why couldn't I think of a better excuse? Oh well. I was actually sneaking in here to steal something back—a book he confiscated from me—but I couldn't exactly admit that." She brightens, adding, "It's a human book he confiscated, by the way. I like your fiction. Well, I've been able to secretly read two of your human fiction books that I found hidden away in the castle, but I liked both of them. Are there more than two? How many fiction books are there?"

"Um . . . lots. Sorry, but why aren't you . . . you know . . ."

I gesture to my neck weakly.

"Oh! Why aren't I killing you?" she suggests brightly.

I nod, swallowing the lump in my throat.

"I'm a vegetarian. The first one ever, you'll be interested to know," she says proudly as her bat flies onto the desk, landing in the inkpot. "So I'm not going to hurt you. And the other vampires of Skeleton Woods stick to a diet of animals, anyway, rather than Goreway residents, not that you're meant to be able to come anywhere near us. My name is Sharptooth Shadow. Nice to meet you!"

She holds out her hand. Staring at it, I eventually take it in mine and we shake hands.

"I'm Maggie," I croak. "Maggie Helsby."

"Well, Maggie Helsby, you're the first person in *years* to make it to the castle, so you must be very impressive. Are you a human hero? There were heroes in those books I read."

"I-I'm not a hero."

"Oh." She looks disappointed for a moment, then shrugs.

71

"Still, it's very cool to meet a human, even if you're not a hero. Do you know what's strange? You don't smell."

"S-sorry?"

"You don't *smell*," she repeats, as though the point she's making is obvious. "Vampires can smell humans from a way off. You know, how a predator can smell its prey?"

I gulp. She continues happily as though she hasn't said anything uncomfortable.

"But you don't smell at all. It's so weird! Count Bloodthirst couldn't smell you even though you were in his bed! That's crazy. He's got the best nose out of everyone. How come vampires can't smell you?"

"I . . . uh . . . how can a vampire be vegetarian?" I ask, ignoring her question, my head whirling.

It's like I'm in a crazy dream. I'm having a conversation with a *vampire*. But I'm starting to believe her when she says she's not going to hurt me.

"I live off beet juice," she sighs, ignoring her bat, who is busy hopping all over blank pieces of parchment, leaving inky bat footprints everywhere. "It's getting a bit boring, to be honest. You know, having beet juice *all* the time. But I'm determined to be vegetarian, so I have to put up with it. I'm fascinated with humans and animals, you see. I'm trying to work out whether there's anything else I can eat other than beet juice, but so far no luck. How did you get to the castle?"

"I just . . . walked."

"Seriously?" She peers at me, fascinated. "You didn't feel anything? The enchantments didn't work at all?"

I shake my head. "Sorry."

"Weird." She looks thoughtful and then claps her hands. "Right! We had better get you out of the castle, before any non-vegetarian vampires spot you. That would be BAD. Technically, they shouldn't hurt you, but you are trespassing and you can't always trust a vampire's willpower, you know? It's not worth the risk. Although, saying that, you can trust me, of course. Bat-Ears, stop messing around. We have to come back and clean here now and you're making it worse."

The bat stops dancing across the parchment and, with a quick flick of his feet to shake the remaining ink off, he swoops up and lands on her shoulder.

"Here," she says, rushing over to the wardrobe in the corner and pulling out a black cloak with a red silk lining. "Put this on."

It swamps me and I have to hold up the bottom so I don't trip, but Sharptooth insists it's better than nothing.

Putting her arm around me and keeping my head low, we wait until Bat-Ears flies into the corridor and gives us the all clear before hurrying out of the study and back across the hall to the door.

Sharptooth stays with me until we're safely out the castle and past the clearing, far out into the darkness of the trees. We keep running and running, faster than I've ever gone before, until I'm completely out of breath and have a horrible stitch. I can't see where we're going because if I look up my eyes water from the speed we're going at. Sharptooth steers me, jolting me this way and that around the twisting tree trunks, until we come to an abrupt halt. I look up and realize that in a matter of seconds we're somehow near the edge of the woods. I can hear the trickle of the stream, near where I left my bike.

"You're safe now," Sharptooth says, taking a step back. "I can't take you any farther because of the sunshine. It would turn me to dust. And that wouldn't be fun. For me, I mean. Maybe for you, though. I've never seen it happen, but it could be quite entertaining!"

"I don't want you to turn to dust. You saved my life," I wheeze, clutching my side. "You're really fast."

"That was just a stroll. You should see what I can really

do," she boasts, putting her hands on her hips. "I didn't want to snap your legs, though, which is what would have happened if I'd run at full speed."

I wince at the idea before untying the cloak from around my neck, rolling it up, and handing it over to her. She tucks it under her arm. "I don't know how to thank you for saving me."

She shrugs. "It's OK. It's been nice meeting you, Maggie Helsby."

"It's been nice meeting you, Sharptooth Shadow." I smile weakly. "Thanks again."

She nods before lifting her cloak and giving it a gigantic swish. It's a bit too dramatic and she stumbles off-balance, getting twisted up in all the material, while her bat is thrown off into the air. He gives an indignant squeak before returning grumpily to her shoulder.

"Whoops," she says to me, sighing. "I really need to start paying attention in class."

And with that, she gives me a wave before bounding away through the trees, disappearing into the mist.

7

"S HE'S ALIVE!"

I almost fall off my bike at Ari's scream, coming to a stop just as I've turned the corner around the hedge, a safe distance from the edge of the woods. Ari and Miles have been waiting for me and, as I swing my leg off my bike, they come racing over.

"We thought you were DEAD," Ari explains, giving me a hug before thumping me on the arm. "WHERE WERE YOU?"

"I was in the woods," I laugh.

"We were just about to go tell your mum and dad," she says, putting her hands on her hips. "We would have been in SO much trouble. Didn't you get our calls?"

"What happened?" Miles asks, his eyes wide with curiosity. "I can't believe you were in the woods for so long! You're so brave."

"I wasn't in there *that* long. And I messaged you saying I was OK."

"Yeah, right before you ignored us for ages," Ari points out. "I felt so bad about leaving you in there! I just got so . . . scared suddenly."

"Me too." Miles nods, shuddering. "I was a little bit nervous going in, but then I got this horrible, cold feeling . . ."

"Same, like my blood turned to ice," Ari jumps in. "It was like I knew something wasn't right and I had to get out of there. As soon as I got back on the bike and started pedaling away, the feeling started to fade. Maggie, weren't you freaked out *at all*?"

"Um." I think about lying in the coffin while Count Bloodthirst paraded about the room. "Yeah, I had my moments."

"So, what happened?" Ari asks eagerly. "Did you see anything strange?"

I hesitate. They wait patiently for my answer, staring at me in awe.

"No," I say eventually, their faces falling with disappointment. "Nothing strange at all."

* * *

I can't stop thinking about what happened. I can't sleep that night or the one after. I lie in bed, wondering if it was all a dream. I stare out my bedroom window for most of the weekend, face pressed against the glass, trying to make out any movement among the trees, but it's perfectly still.

I met a vampire. A VAMPIRE.

I'm not sure exactly why I didn't tell Ari and Miles the truth about finding the castle and meeting Sharptooth. I guess because it sounds so crazy, I'm not sure they'd believe me. But there's another reason, too. Part of me felt strangely *protective*; I had this overwhelming feeling that I should keep it secret. That I didn't want to ruin any of it.

Which doesn't make any sense at all.

Maybe it's because Sharptooth saved me when she didn't have to, and now I want to keep her safe, too. Who knows what the town would do if they realized that vampires really do exist?

The following week at school, I wander about in a daze for days, too distracted to concentrate on any lessons or anything going on around me. At least three teachers tell me off for being in a daydream when I'm supposed to be on a certain page of whatever textbook they're talking about, but I don't care. I sit in classrooms all day every day, lost in thought about Sharptooth Shadow and how . . . *nice* she was.

A vegetarian vampire? Is that even a thing? Maybe it really was a dream. Maybe I made it all up in my head. The castle, Sharptooth, Count Bloodthirst . . . all of it. Maybe I passed out in the woods, had a strange dream about vampires, and then woke up.

But it seemed so *real*.

"Hello! Earth to Maggie!"

A fry hits me square on the forehead, landing on my lunch tray. I blink across the table at Ari.

"Sorry," I say hurriedly, picking up my fork and stabbing at my lunch. "What were you saying?"

"I was saying you've been acting strange all week," she tells me, stealing another fry from Miles's plate, but this time to eat rather than throw at me. "Is everything OK?"

"Yeah," I assure her, smiling as broadly as possible. "Everything's fine! I'm just overwhelmed by all the homework we've been given."

"Me too," Miles sighs. "I feel so behind."

Ari snorts, nudging him with her elbow. "Whatever, Miles. We all know you're top of the class, so don't try to pretend that you're like us. You probably want *more* homework, knowing you."

As they launch into one of their familiar squabbles, I look down at my food, willing myself to be hungry. But like every mealtime for the past few days, I barely touch it, too tired and distracted to eat.

I can't keep going like this. I can't focus on normal life after last weekend. I need to know if it was real. I want to see Sharptooth again. I have too many questions clouding my brain, and she's the only person who can answer them. There's only one thing for it.

I have to go back to Skeleton Woods.

That evening, I jump over the stream and walk into the shadows of the trees, listening out for any movement. I'm a little more on edge this time around, knowing that there are vampires potentially lurking about, but I keep going, determined not to chicken out.

It's impossible to walk silently, twigs and leaves crunching under my sneakers, but I try to be as quiet as possible all the same, slowly and carefully making my way in the same direction as last time. Once I'm through the mist, I stop and lean back against a tree, wondering if I've lost my mind.

I probably should have come up with a plan. How am I

even going to find Sharptooth? How will I get her attention without any of the others noticing? Didn't she say something about *hundreds of vampires* in the castle?

I bite my lip, jumping at every sound. Earlier I found it funny when I decided the best time to come here had to be as the evening drew in, so it would be dark enough for a vampire not to worry about the sun and light enough for a human to be able to see through the woods—twilight. Of course. The best time to go hunt a vampire was always going to be twilight. Now that I'm here, I'm not sure how funny it was after all. Daytime seems much more sensible. And the leaves and branches of the trees in Skeleton Woods make such a thick canopy, it's always dark in here anyway. I should have waited for the weekend and come here during the day, when I had the option of running away into the sunshine.

"Come on, Maggie," I whisper to myself, taking a deep breath. "You're brave. You have to keep going."

I stand up straight, steeling myself. I take one step around the tree and walk straight into someone.

"AHHHHHHHHH!" I scream, stumbling backward.

My foot catches on a tree branch and I'm about to fall to the ground, but Sharptooth grabs my wrist, pulling me back with ease and letting me regain my balance.

"It's me!" she says, letting go of my hand and giving me a wave. "Remember? The vegetarian vampire!"

I lean on the tree, catching my breath. "Sharptooth. I'm so glad it's you."

"What are you doing here?" she asks, her eyes wide with excitement. "It's very risky coming back."

"I know," I say, taking in her long sweeping cloak, fangs, and red eyes. Bat-Ears hangs from her elbow, fast asleep.

I didn't dream it. It was all real. *I knew it.*

"I thought you might be back," she says proudly. "I could sense it. You kept staring at the woods every night from your window."

"I . . . uh . . . you could see that?"

"Vampires have great eyesight," she tells me eagerly, opening her red eyes nice and wide to emphasize her point. "We have great everything, to be honest. We're vastly superior creatures to humans. I don't mean that nastily or anything."

"Right." I nod, finding myself smiling at her.

"Anyway, that's how I knew to come find you here. I saw you gazing at the woods and I thought to myself, *She's going to come back here soon*, so I've been looking out for you a lot, just in case. And then just now I saw you coming home from school, but you weren't being driven by your parents like normal, you were walking home and you were very jumpy. You ducked behind the hedge and ran along the path toward the woods, and I thought to myself, *She's told her parents a lie and they think she's somewhere else right now, that's why they haven't picked her up from school.*"

My smile gets bigger and I start to relax as she continues chattering away.

"I decided I'd come meet you before any other vampires realized you were here in the woods. I waited a bit, though, because I didn't want to scare you straight away. When you came and stood by this tree, I was worried you might change your mind and go home. And I wanted to say hello before you did. I hope I didn't scare you too much?" She grimaces apologetically. "It's hard not to scare a human when you're a vampire."

"Sure." I grin. "But you don't need to worry, you didn't scare me too much. Thanks for coming to meet me."

She folds her arms, Bat-Ears swinging as she moves. "What are you doing here, Maggie Helsby? It's very dangerous."

"I thought I might have dreamed it all," I explain, gesturing at her. "I wanted to make sure you were real."

She nods thoughtfully. "I am real."

"I can see."

"It's so weird that you don't smell."

"In the human world, that's a good thing."

She tilts her head. "But you all have such potent individual scents."

"We do?"

"Yes. And all of them are *very* tasty. I'm sure if you had a smell, it would be tasty, too."

"Oh. Cool. Thanks."

"You're welcome."

"You're . . . uh . . . definitely vegetarian, right?"

"Definitely. You don't need to worry. I promise."

I hesitate before swinging my backpack off my shoulder and unzipping the top. "I brought you something."

I reach into my bag and pull out a well-thumbed book.

When I made up my mind to come back here and try to find Sharptooth, I remembered what she'd said about how much she liked fiction and how she'd only ever read two books, so I thought it would be a nice gesture to bring another one for her. You know, just in case she turned out to not be as vegetarian as I remembered. I thought I could give her the book as a peace offering.

I went to the school library this afternoon and stood among the shelves for what felt like forever.

"What book would a vampire like to read?" I muttered under my breath, scanning the rows of colorful spines.

I was getting very annoyed at myself for being so indecisive when a title jumped out at me.

"Here," I say, holding it out for her. "Have you read this?"

Her jaw drops open in surprise and she takes the book in her hands as though it's the most precious thing in the whole world.

"*Matilda* by Roald Dahl," she says, reading the title aloud before looking up at me. "I haven't read this one. Is it one of your human fiction books?"

"Yeah." I nod, smiling at her as she strokes the cover with her sharp, pointed fingernail. "I thought you'd like it because it's about a girl who loves books and feels like she's a bit out of place. I figured you might feel the same sometimes. It must be hard for you being the only vegetarian vampire and, well, you know . . ."

I trail off, not sure how best to explain, but it doesn't matter. She hugs the book to her chest.

"Thank you, Maggie Helsby."

"No worries. It's actually on loan from the library, so

you have it for two weeks and then I can return it and get you another one to read. If you want."

"Another fiction book?"

"Yeah."

She looks like she might keel over from excitement. "I need to give you something in return."

"No, no," I say, zipping my bag back up, "you really don't—"

"I want to." She gasps, an idea popping into her brain. "Wait right here. Don't move." She turns to go, stopping to look over her shoulder at me. "And don't get eaten by any of my fellow vampires. You should be OK—we're not supposed to wander around this far out, but you never know. Count Bloodthirst sometimes likes to walk around the woods for peace and quiet. So, avoid a tall, old vampire in a cloak with big sharp teeth."

"Right. Will do."

She sets off, running so fast that she becomes a blur. I stare in wonder at the empty space where she was standing, amazed at her speed. I'm just getting over it when she appears in front of me again.

"Whoa," I breathe. "How do you run so fast?"

"I'm a vampire," she answers simply. Bat-Ears is still

asleep, hanging from her sleeve, apparently undisturbed by the speed of light at which they'd moved. "I thought I'd bring you something from the vampire world, as you've brought me something from the human one."

"Great," I say, grimacing. "Uh . . . it's not a . . . severed hand or anything, is it?"

"No," she says, suddenly worried. "Why, is that what you'd like?"

"No, no, definitely not."

"Oh good. I didn't even *think* of that."

She holds out her hand. Lying in the middle of her palm is what can only be described as a small piece of rock.

"Wow," I say as enthusiastically as I can muster, searching for the words. "It's . . . it's a pebble."

"It's a piece of the stone wall from the castle. It chipped off my bedroom last week when Bat-Ears and I were wrestling and I bumped into the wall."

I glance at the tiny Bat-Ears and then back up at her, frowning in confusion. "You were wrestling with a bat?"

"Do humans not wrestle with bats?"

I shake my head.

"I'm not surprised," she sighs. "Bats are very strong. Bat-Ears is VICIOUS."

Bat-Ears wakes for a moment, stretching out his wings, revealing his fluffy little belly. He eyes me suspiciously upside down before yawning and wrapping himself back up in his wings, snoring gently.

"OK," I say simply. "I'll take your word for it."

"The reason I'm giving you this bit of rock from the castle wall is so that you have proof," she explains. "You said you weren't sure if you'd been dreaming before. Now, whenever you wonder, you can look at this rock and know that it was all real."

I reach out and take the piece of rock from her ice-cold hand, closing my fingers around it. I can't believe I was so dismissive of this stone when she first held it out.

"Do you like it?" she asks. "Are you happy with your present?"

"Sharptooth, this is the best and *coolest* present anyone has EVER given me," I say, grinning at her. "I mean it. I love my present. Thank you."

She looks overwhelmed by my heartfelt answer. Her whole body tenses and the corners of her mouth start twitching, her eyes wide with panic.

"Are you OK?" I ask.

"Something . . . something's happening to my face,"

she says. "My mouth is . . . it's turning upward!"

"Yeah," I say, bewildered by her overreaction. "You're smiling."

"I . . . I am?" she whispers, her hands flying to her face. "I'm *smiling*? Are you sure? I've never . . . I've never done that before!"

"You've never smiled before?"

"Vampires don't do that! We're not supposed to smile. But it feels so nice!"

I burst out laughing as she continues to pat her jaw in utter amazement.

"I can't believe I'm smiling," she whispers. "Maggie, how do I look?"

Her fangs are on full display, her eyes full of wonder.

"Sharptooth," I begin, super excited to say what I'm about to say and mean it LITERALLY, "you look absolutely *fang-tastic*."

I t's your turn," Sharptooth announces happily, sipping from a bottle of beet juice through a red-striped straw, sitting cross-legged in front of me while Bat-Ears entertains himself by kicking up the leaves from the woodland floor.

"OK, next question I have for you is this," I say, leaning back against a tree trunk. "Do vampires have to wear cloaks *all* the time?"

"Yes," she says, putting her drink down. "Count Bloodthirst insists that it's key to the vampire look. I'm not sure if it's the same in other countries, though."

"Are there vampires in every country in the world?"

"It's *my* turn to ask a question, Maggie," she points out. "One each, remember? Don't try to sneak in another one without me noticing."

I laugh, holding up my hands. "All right, your turn."

We came up with this rule last time I was here—today is my fourth venture into Skeleton Woods. I obviously have a BILLION questions about vampires and it turns out she has just as many about humans, so we thought that taking turns to ask each other a question was a fair system.

I look forward to hanging out with Sharptooth more than anything else. I have to keep it completely secret, and I do feel bad lying to my parents about where I am. But it's worth it. I can't believe I get to spend time with a VAMPIRE.

She tried to talk me out of it at first. After she gave me the bit of rock from the castle, she told me I should keep out of the woods, just like the signs around the edge say.

"You're very lucky that I was the one to find you in Count Bloodthirst's office," she pointed out. "And I'm pleased I was looking out for you this time. But what if I hadn't been? What if you'd bumped into Count Bloodthirst on one of his bird-watching walks?"

"Bird-watching? I thought you said he walks through the woods for some peace and quiet."

"Yes, and to bird-watch. Is that another thing humans don't do?"

"Actually, bird-watching is a thing," I confirmed. "I just

can't imagine someone like Count Bloodthirst enjoys that sort of hobby when he's so . . . so . . ."

"Evil?" Sharptooth offered eagerly.

"Well, yeah." I shrugged.

"Evil vampires enjoy lots of hobbies. There's a vampire called Deathfoot who likes smashing things."

"Oh, OK," I said, not sure if that really counted as a hobby but not keen to argue it out with a vampire, even a vegetarian one. "Anyway, I know it was dangerous to come here, but I needed to know for sure."

"You shouldn't come here again," she said solemnly. "You seem like a nice human, and I don't want you to get hurt."

"Me neither. But I can come hang out with you, right? I have a LOT of questions, and you'll need to return the book."

She looked thoughtful. "I guess I have a lot of questions about humans, too. Like, what does the sunshine feel like on your face?"

"Warm."

"Must be nice to walk in the sunshine and not turn to dust."

"That is nice. But hey, must be cool to run fast as light and be super strong."

She replied it was pretty fun, and after that it didn't take much persuading to get her to agree to meet again in the same spot the next day at the same time. She said that it was a good time to meet because it was when Count Bloodthirst was usually busy with Cackle Class, so we were safe.

"How come you're not in Cackle Class?" I asked.

"I've already learned how to cackle," she said proudly. "I don't need any more lessons."

"I thought that vampires weren't supposed to smile. How can they cackle without smiling?"

"Like this!" she cried, thrilled to have the opportunity to show off.

She demonstrated her best evil vampire cackle and it genuinely chilled me to the bone. She then encouraged me to give it a go, but my attempt didn't go so well. She gave me a strange look and asked if I'd meant to do an impression of a cute, fluffy kitten.

Last time we met, I grilled her about her diet and her age. The first thing I wanted to know was whether she ever felt tempted to quit the whole vegetarian thing, but she assured me that she was committed to the cause. Then, when my turn came around again to ask a question, I asked why she's such a young vampire when Count Bloodthirst is older. She explained that vampires stay the age they are when they're turned into a vampire. She was twelve years old and Count Bloodthirst had been sixty-eight. Vampires don't live forever, she said, but they age very slowly.

I wanted to ask how long she'd been a vampire and whether she remembered anything about her human life, but then I realized the time and I knew if I didn't get home, my parents would lose it.

I'm waiting for a good moment to bring it back up today. They're the kind of questions I don't think I can just blurt out straight away.

"I've thought of my question," Sharptooth says, twisting the straw around in her bottle. "What is *music?*"

I blink at her. "Huh?"

"Music. What is it?" She shrugs as Bat-Ears gives up with the leaves and hops into her lap. "I've read about it in those three books. It's something that humans do or like or something."

"Wait a second." I lean forward. "You don't know what music is?"

She shakes her head.

"OK, that's ridiculous." I run a hand through my hair.

"Music is very hard to explain. It's a sound . . . well, a series of sounds, I guess. And a beat. And you listen to it."

"Sound and beat," she says, her forehead furrowed as she concentrates. "What do you mean by beat? Like a human heartbeat?"

"Yeah, sort of. You know what? The best way of explaining music is to let you listen to some."

I get my headphones from my backpack and pass them to her. She looks up at me blankly.

"Is this music?"

"They're headphones," I laugh, shuffling across to her and showing her how to put them on. "It's how you listen. Do you have super-good hearing?"

"It's not your turn to ask a question."

"No, that wasn't one of my questions. I just need to know because I don't want the volume to be up too loud."

She looks at me suspiciously, her hands holding the headphones as though worried they'll suddenly crush her head. "Yes, we have very good hearing."

"I'll turn this right down, then," I say, scrolling through my playlists on my phone. "You can always tell me if you want it louder."

"Do I need to do anything?" Sharptooth asks.

"Nope. Just sit there and listen."

It's a lot of pressure to pick the first song to play to someone who has never heard music before. I decide to go with an uplifting, happy pop song that I'm obsessed with at the moment because it's a very summery tune and she'd asked that question about sunshine, so I thought she might like it.

I press play.

As the music starts, she jumps in shock and then stays frozen still, her hands clamped on the headphones. By the time the chorus comes in, her mouth is twitching into her unusual smile again, her face lighting up with joy.

She looks up at me, her red eyes gleaming. "I don't want it to end."

I laugh as I watch her expressions change throughout the song. I've never seen anyone look so unashamedly happy before. At moments like this, it's easy to forget she's a vampire.

She pulls off the headphones when the song finishes and hands them back to me reluctantly.

"That was *wonderful*," she emphasizes. "No wonder humans are obsessed with it."

"There are thousands of songs, all different genres, too."

"Thousands?" She shakes her head in amazement. "Are they all as good as that one?"

I smile to myself, shoving the headphones away in my bag. "Some of them are even better. But it all depends on what you like. People like different things."

"I wonder what music *I* like," she says excitedly. "I want to listen to all of it."

I hesitate. "Sharptooth, I have my next question ready."

"Go ahead."

"Do you . . . do you remember anything about being a human? You know, before you were . . . before you became a vampire."

"No, nothing," she tells me with a shrug. "My memories start from the day I woke up as a vampire after Count Bloodthirst turned me. It's the same for all vampires. I do know that I was an orphan, though."

"Count Bloodthirst told you that."

"Actually, no," she says. "The prophecy told me that."

"Prophecy?" I lean toward her, enraptured. "There's a *prophecy*? About you?"

"Yes," she says glumly, stroking Bat-Ears's tiny head with her little finger.

"What does it say?"

"It says that I'm the Chosen Leader."

"The WHAT?"

"The Chosen Leader," she repeats, her eyebrows knitted together. "Every hundred years, the vampire leader reads a prophecy that guides them to the human who will take over from them once they're turned into a vampire and trained up. Count Bloodthirst is the current Chosen Leader and, according to the prophecy he read, I'm the next one. That's why he gets so cross at me when I don't listen in class. There's a lot of expectation. Also, the vegetarian decision hasn't gone down very well in the community."

"I can imagine," I say quietly.

"Everyone thinks that the prophecy somehow messed up. I'm not Chosen Leader material. I can't even swish my cloak properly. How am I supposed to lead vampires to greatness?"

I suddenly feel guilty about stressing over small things like being behind on homework. At least I don't have to worry about fulfilling a prophecy. I watch her as she strokes Bat-Ear's head gloomily. She's so naturally cheerful, it doesn't seem right to see her looking so down. I shouldn't have asked her about all this.

"Let's listen to some more music," I suggest brightly,

reaching for my headphones again. "We have LOTS to get through. I'll have to ask Ari and Miles to put together a list of the best songs of all time for me. They know a lot more about music than I do."

Sharptooth tilts her head. "Who are Ari and Miles?"

"They're my friends from school."

"Oh." She nods. "Vampires aren't supposed to have friends."

"I guess that makes sense," I say, scrolling through some playlist suggestions, looking for a good one, while Sharptooth sits deep in thought.

"Maggie, I've thought of my next question," she says suddenly.

"Sure, it's your turn. What do you want to know?"

"Do you think *we're* friends?"

I look up from my phone to see her staring at me hopefully.

"Yeah, Sharptooth. We're friends."

She picks the headphones up happily, places them over her ears, and then leans back against the tree with her eyes closed, ready to listen to some music, her bat contentedly falling asleep on her shoulder.

I t's Maggie, isn't it?"

I look up to see Mr. Frank, the school librarian, standing at the end of the row smiling at me. I decided to spend the morning break in between lessons hunting down some more books in the library, desperate to find out as much as possible about Skeleton Woods.

I also needed to work out the next book to give Sharptooth once she is done with her current read. It's hard to know what to choose for a vampire who is new to fiction.

"Yes, hi, Mr. Frank," I reply, sliding a book back into its slot in the history section. "Sorry, am I not meant to be in here?"

"You are always welcome in a library," he says, brushing aside my silly comment with a wave of his hand. "I've just noticed that you've been here a few times since starting at

100

the school and I wondered if you wanted any help in picking your next book."

"That would be great, thank you!"

His expression lights up, thrilled to be able to help, and he comes over to join me in front of the history rows. From the few times I've been in the library, I've worked out that Mr. Frank is a very smiley person, because whenever I've strolled through the doors, he's looked up from his desk with a warm, happy expression. He's in his late thirties, I think, and has very messy, curly brown hair and bold, dark eyebrows, and he's always smartly dressed in a shirt and tie.

He seems to have a good sense of humor, too, because the other day he was walking across the schoolyard and someone kicked a soccer ball up in the air that accidentally hit him on the back of the head. He turned around, stunned, before launching into a hilarious, over-the-top performance of falling to the ground, lying there like a starfish. The students all gave him a big round of applause, during which he jumped up and took a flourishing bow before shoving his hands back into his pockets and sauntering away.

"What exactly are you after?" he asks, coming to stand next to me. "Is it something for your history class?"

"Uh . . . no. I'm actually interested in *local* history."

He raises his eyebrows. "Oh?"

"Do you have anything about Goreway? Skeleton Woods, in particular."

"Ah." He grins. "Miss Woods told me that you were interested in the horror genre. You've moved to the right town, that's for sure. I'm not sure anywhere matches the sort of spooky tales we have here in Goreway."

"I've read a lot online about it," I tell him excitedly. "But not much that goes into the full detail about the woods. And a lot of the blogs I've read talk about the mysteries of what's in the woods, but don't seem to have many real-life tales or accounts from Goreway residents of the past."

He crouches down to scan the books on the bottom shelf. "I suppose that partly comes from the fact that, if the rumors are to be believed, when you go into the woods, you don't come out."

He chuckles at the idea. I laugh along with him, before gulping at the thought of someone coming across Count Bloodthirst in the dead of night . . .

"Here you go," he says, beckoning for me to crouch down next to him, "this bottom row here is everything we have on local history." He hesitates, examining the spine of one of the books and sliding it out. "What is your surname again, Maggie?"

"Helsby."

He blinks at me. "That's strange. The author of this book on the history of Goreway is someone named Mina Helsby! A relation, perhaps?"

He holds it out for me and I take it, astonished to see my surname printed in bold letters above the title of the book. The date on the inside cover reveals the book was first published in 1903.

"I have no idea," I admit, flicking through the pages. "I thought our only link to Goreway was my great-uncle Bram. He lived in Skeleton Lodge before us."

"You live in Skeleton Lodge?" Mr. Frank's eyes widen in fascination as I nod. "So, you're very close to the woods, then. Maybe . . . uh . . . maybe it's not such a good idea for you to read the history."

"If you think I'll find it too scary, you don't need to worry. I won't," I say with a shrug, selecting two more books from the shelf. "The scarier the better in my opinion."

He looks impressed. "If you say so. Just don't go getting nightmares from books I've led you to, otherwise Miss Woods won't be amused."

"Trust me, you don't need to worry." I straighten up, pleased with the pile of books in my arms. "Mr. Frank, can I ask you something?"

"Sure," he says, standing up properly again.

"On my first day here, Miss Woods mentioned that the school has a mysterious tale, but she didn't have time to go into detail. Is that true?"

"Oh yes." He nods eagerly, gesturing for me to follow him back down the row toward his desk. "In fact, I think one or two of the books you've chosen there should outline some of the legendary tales about Goreway School, but I also have . . . hang on."

He steps around his desk and starts pulling open the drawers one by one, each of them filled to the brim with jumbled papers and old notebooks, until he discovers the book he's after in the bottom drawer and holds it up triumphantly. I can see from its title that it's a comprehensive history of Goreway School and its architecture.

"Here, you can borrow this, too," he says, putting it on top of the pile of books that I set down on his desk. "This book devotes a full chapter to the last known resident of this building, Mr. Arthur Quince. I imagine that Miss Woods was referring to him when she spoke about 'mysterious tales' of the school. When I first came to the school, I thought it would be a good idea to read up about its history and, I have to admit, I was not expecting such an unusual background."

"Who was Arthur Quince?"

"Mr. Arthur Quince was a very wealthy gentleman who lived in the town a long time ago, in the 1800s," Mr. Frank begins, taking a seat and clasping his hands together, "and, before it became a school, this was his house."

"Wait, the ENTIRE school was this guy's house?" I ask in disbelief as Mr. Frank nods. "Whoa. It's massive! He must have been really rich."

"He was, and, by all accounts, he was very generous, too," Mr. Frank continues. "Apparently, he was well-liked by a lot of people in the town and much respected. He was known as an intelligent, sensible man. Which makes the circumstances of his story all the more strange."

"What happened to him?"

"One night, Arthur Quince was returning from his travels on horseback. This was, according to reports by those who knew him at the time, not unusual. He was a keen horseman. This night, for reasons unknown, he decided to take a different route home, a path that led alongside Skeleton Woods."

"I can already tell this is going to be good," I say, leaning on his desk, completely enraptured.

Mr. Frank smiles, his eyes twinkling as he tells the story, his voice taking on a spooky tone, just like Ari's and mine did when we were trying to scare Miles in the tent.

"Suddenly, as he nears the trees, his horse comes to a halt, refusing to go any farther. As it's dark, Quince thinks she may have been spooked by something in front of her, so he hops down and goes to inspect the path to see, but there's nothing there. Even so, the horse seems to get another fright and bolts off into the darkness. She ran all the way home, leaving Quince stranded by the woodland. That was when he saw them."

He pauses for dramatic effect.

"Saw what?" I ask dutifully, although I have a sneaking suspicion I already know.

"A pair of red eyes watching him from the darkness of the woods." Mr. Frank must be waiting for me to gasp at this point as he looks up at me expectantly, but I don't react, so he clears his throat and continues, trying to hide his disappointment. "Anyway, there right ahead of him are these eyes staring right at him. And next thing he knows, the person they belong to steps forward. The figure is deathly pale and Quince can see, glinting in the moonlight, their two white fangs."

Again, he pauses.

"So . . . a vampire," I prompt impatiently. "What next?"

"Yes, well, um, this vampire steps forward and, as you can imagine, Quince is frozen in fear. He can't move. He tries to scream but no sound comes out. The vampire begins to approach him and he can see it's thirsty, but then . . . a miracle. A man appears at Quince's side."

"Who was it?" I ask, furrowing my brow.

"He didn't know." Mr. Frank shrugs. "A mysterious man that Quince had never seen before. And he thought he knew the majority of people in the town, but this man he'd never seen in his life. The man is carrying a flaming torch and he holds it up, so that the light flickers on the vampire's face. And then he spoke to the vampire—and this is the strange part—*as though he knew him.*"

Now I gasp. Mr. Frank looks pleased that his story has had some effect at last. But he couldn't possibly understand the reason behind my surprise at that last detail. If this is in any way true, I might not be the first person to stumble upon the vampire community in Skeleton Woods and live to tell the tale.

"What did he say?" I demand to know.

"There are many different accounts of the exact words spoken, as you can imagine," Mr. Frank sighs. "It was a long time ago and who knows how reliable the reports from the time were? But something about how the vampire knew the consequences if he took one more step toward Quince. He didn't say much, just a few words, but whatever they were, they did the job."

"What do you mean?"

"The vampire disappeared back into the woods."

I frown. "No way. Just because a man with a flaming torch tells him that there will be consequences, the vampire flees? That can't be right. Are you sure?"

"Don't shoot the messenger," Mr. Frank laughs, holding up his hands. "This is how the story goes. Quince was saved by a mysterious man and a few choice words. And if that doesn't make much sense to you, get this—according to Quince, the vampire didn't just stop and listen. He looked *frightened*."

"He was frightened by the mysterious man?"

Mr. Frank nods. "That's right. The torch is blown out by the swishing of the vampire's cloak as he spins around and flees. Quince turns to thank the man for saving his life, but he's gone, too. Disappeared into the night. Quince never got his name or had the chance to thank him. That was it."

"Who WAS this man?" I ask, baffled.

"No one knows. And poor Quince is left reeling from the night's events, overwhelmed by what's just happened. So he runs as fast as he can home, stumbles into town, and wakes everyone up. He shouts and screams, running down the main street, banging on doors, yelling at the top of his lungs. The townspeople start coming out of their houses into the street, wondering what's going on, and there's the respectable Arthur Quince crying out that they all need to leave the town straight away because they're under attack from vampires. You can imagine how that went down."

I bite my lip, concerned for Quince, even though this happened so long ago. "I'm guessing they didn't believe him?"

"He told them all the story. He told them several times exactly what had happened. The horse bolting, the vampire appearing, the mystery man who frightened the vampire away. At first they all thought Quince was playing a bizarre trick, some kind of joke, but when they realized he was being serious, when they saw the fear on his face, they started to understand that Quince believed every word he was saying. They laughed in his face. Everyone went home and he was left shouting his warnings all alone in the street. And the next morning, he was gone."

"Gone home?"

"Nope, gone from the town," Mr. Frank reveals. "No one ever saw him again. His house—this very building—was completely untouched. His clothes and all his belongings were still here. The staff who lived in the house slept through the night without being disturbed and woke the next morning to find that their master's bedroom was empty, his bed still made. He had not returned home. No one saw or heard from him again."

"Hang on, he just . . . disappeared?"

"Some say he was so spooked that he took as much of his money he could carry and went as far away as possible, never wanting to return to Goreway. Others say he decided to return to the woods to try to find that man again so he had proof of his story. Maybe the vampire was lying in wait for him. Nobody knows. All we know for sure is that this house was left with no one to live in it and many, many years later, after it became clear that no one was coming to claim it, it was turned into a school. And here we are."

"Right." I nod slowly, taking it all in. "He just disappeared."

"I think in Mina Helsby's book she addresses the rumors that his ghost still haunts the school—" Mr. Frank hesitates, looking up at me in concern. "Are you sure you're not scared by any of this? I don't want you reading anything that makes you feel nervous or uncomfortable about coming to school."

"Why would his ghost still haunt the school?" I ask, ignoring his thoughtful but silly question. "Surely, his spirit wouldn't return to his house. The house didn't have much to do with the story about the vampire."

Mr. Frank blinks at me. "Well . . . maybe . . . he felt safest here? Rather than near the woods. That's why his ghost would want to return here. To be safe."

"Hmm. Maybe," I say, flipping Mina Helsby's book open and examining the chapter headings. "I hope there's lots of information in here about Arthur Quince."

"I don't think you'll be disappointed," Mr. Frank laughs, logging into his computer to sort out my loans. "You'll have to let me know how you get on with these books."

"I will. Thank you so much for all your help."

"Any time."

When he's done, I pick up the stack of books, thank him for the brilliant storytelling, and start to make my way toward the exit of the library as the bell goes for the start of the next lesson. I stop at the door and turn to face him.

"Mr. Frank?"

"Yes, Maggie?" he says, looking up from his computer screen.

"Do you believe Arthur Quince? You know, his tale of events about . . . about seeing a real vampire. Would you . . . believe any of that?"

"Do I believe that there's a vampire out there, roaming Skeleton Woods?" He laughs, shaking his head. "No, Maggie, I don't. Please don't worry about it."

"It's not that, I'm not worried or scared. I just—"

"Look at it this way," Mr. Frank continues, keen to comfort me and clearly not believing my claims that I haven't been spooked by his story, "if there was a vampire in Skeleton Woods, why haven't they come out of the woods at night into the town? Why would a vampire stay in Skeleton Woods when there's a town of people just down the road?"

I nod. "I suppose. Except, there was that man. The one

who frightened the vampire away, he protected the towns-people. Who was he?"

"Goreway's guardian angel, maybe." Mr. Frank grins as the second school bell rings. "Or much more likely, a figment of Mr. Arthur Quince's imagination."

A ri and Miles are getting suspicious.

Last weekend, they asked me if I wanted to do another tent sleepover and I had to make something up about why I couldn't, because I'd promised to see Sharptooth that night and it's not like I could text her to rearrange.

And tonight I'm due to meet Sharptooth again, and it just so happens that the Goreway movie theater is doing an evening showing of an old zombie film that Ari thought would be right up my street, so, just as I was heading out of school for the day, she and Miles caught up with me and suggested we all get tickets.

"Sorry, I can't," I said hurriedly, feeling a pang of guilt at Ari's disappointed expression. "I have too much homework to do."

"That's a good point," Miles chipped in eagerly, while Ari rolled her eyes. "We could do a study group instead?"

"I . . . uh . . . I can't do that, either. My parents are doing a big celebratory dinner this evening, you know, because the dental practice got new . . . uh . . . drills. Yeah, it's a big deal in the dental world, apparently. Ha ha. So, I have to be there for that. While also doing my homework."

"Oh," Miles said. "Fair enough."

Ari narrowed her eyes at me. "What are you keeping from us?"

"What?"

"I have a nose for these things," Ari declared proudly, crossing her arms. "I can tell that you, Maggie Helsby, have a secret. So, come on, fill us in."

"I don't have a secret!" I protested, my cheeks growing hot with the lie. "What kind of secret would I have?"

"I don't know, but ever since we went into Skeleton Woods you've been acting . . ." She trailed off.

"Acting what?" I prompted, needing to know what it was so I could make sure I wasn't doing it in the future.

"Acting *differently*," she concluded. "Distracted all the time. Are you sure you didn't see anything in there?"

I swallowed the lump in my throat as she leaned in toward me, refusing to break eye contact.

"I'm sure," I croaked, lifting my chin up in the hope it

made me look a lot more confident than I felt. "I really am sorry about tonight, but how about we do something tomorrow night instead? I promise I won't have a dental celebratory dinner to go to tomorrow."

After a few moments of staring me down, Ari nodded slowly, deciding to let it go. "All right, then. We'll hang out tomorrow after school."

It's not very nice lying to friends. I haven't really had any before, so I'm new to this experience, but it doesn't seem like the best thing to do. I'm still feeling guilty about it as I quietly make my way through the mist and trees of Skeleton Woods that evening, spotting Sharptooth sitting at the foot of a tree while Bat-Ears prances about in front of her, flapping his wings. Her mouth twitches into a smile as she sees me approaching.

"Hello, Maggie," she says, waving. "Bat-Ears is practicing his evil entrance. He's really improving, I think. Want to see?"

"What's an evil entrance?" I ask, sitting down cross-legged opposite her.

"You know when a vampire suddenly enters a room, being all evil?"

"I guess I can imagine it."

"Well," she continues cheerily, "a vampire's bat is supposed to enter with them and be equally as menacing and vicious. Bat-Ears has been told that his performance is . . . um . . . not as good as it could be."

"Who said that?"

"Count Bloodthirst," she sighs. "According to him, Bat-Ears should strike fear into the heart of anyone who meets him, human or vampire. But apparently, he's missing the mark. What did you think when you first saw Bat-Ears? You must have been frightened of him!"

"Um." I recall the first time I met Sharptooth in Count Bloodthirst's office and how Bat-Ears dipped his cute little bat toes in ink and left little paw prints all over the desk. "To be honest, I think I was a little more distracted by the vampire with fangs right in front of me."

"Oh dear," Sharptooth says as Bat-Ears swivels around to glare at me. "I'm not sure that's the answer he wanted to hear."

"Why don't you show me your evil entrance, Bat-Ears?" I suggest enthusiastically. "Then I can tell you if it's got even . . . eviller than when I first met you."

Sharptooth nods at Bat-Ears in encouragement. He wraps his wings around himself tightly and then suddenly releases them and pushes himself up into the air, hovering just in front of me. I wait for something more to happen. Nothing does.

"What do you think?" Sharptooth asks me.

"Uh," I say, playing for time as Bat-Ears waits for a review. "It's definitely better. Much better. I just . . . um . . . I wonder if there's any more you can do to be a bit more . . . threatening?"

Bat-Ears looks pensive for a moment, then suddenly zips closer to my face in what I assume is supposed to be a threatening manner, his wings flapping, his fluffy little belly on display.

"Aw." I instinctively smile, reaching out to tickle his belly with my finger. "You're so *cute*."

He recoils from my reach and lets out a piercing, outraged screech before fluttering quickly up to the branch above Sharptooth's head, where he stomps his feet and then drops forward to hang upside down, hiding his face grumpily under his wings.

"Sorry, Bat-Ears," I say, grimacing as I realize my mistake. "When I said cute, I meant . . . evil."

"Don't worry about it; it's probably because his entrance right now is missing the shock factor," Sharptooth reasons.

"He can practice for when you next come into the woods and then jump out and scare the life out of you!"

"Sure. That sounds fun for me."

"I've been so excited to see you again, Maggie," Sharptooth says, her red eyes gleaming. "Because you're my *friend*."

"Me too." I smile.

"I was very distracted in Dribble Class today because I knew I would get to see my FRIEND later. I spilled beet juice all over Maggothead's cloak. He was furious. He'd only just washed it, he said, and for the first time ever had used fabric softener. He was very proud of himself. I told him that he should be pleased I'd given him another excuse to use fabric softener again. But he didn't agree and shouted at me a lot." She shakes her head in grave disappointment. "I've told Maggothead so many times that he needs to watch his temper. Will he listen? No. You may not believe this, Maggie, but some vampires can have a very nasty streak."

"Oh, I believe it."

"I offered to wash his cloak for him as an apology, but Count Bloodthirst says vampires don't apologize, especially the Chosen Leader. Which is strange, because Count

Bloodthirst makes me apologize to him all the time when I'm in trouble."

"What's Dribble Class?" I ask curiously.

"We practice our dribbling technique; you know, when you let blood trickle down your chin after eating so that you look even scarier to those who see you," she reveals cheerily. "Vampires are naturally very neat with their food. The whole blood-dripping-from-the-mouth is just for dramatic effect."

"Right," I say, my hand instinctively flying to my neck and giving it a comforting rub.

"Of course, I use beet juice in my dribble lessons, which actually stains more. So if ever you have the choice between blood and beet juice, keep that in mind."

"Will do. Anyway," I say hurriedly, keen to change the subject, "I've been distracted in my school lessons, too. I've been doing a lot of reading about Skeleton Woods, learning about its history, but most of it is just people guessing. I wondered if you knew more about the vampire side of things?"

"Sure!" she says, kicking the leaves around her feet. "What do you want to know?"

"There's a famous story about a count who tried to

overthrow the King of England centuries ago and then got left in this castle as punishment. According to legend, he was cursed and became a vampire and that's how the vampire community came to be here in Skeleton Woods. Is that true?"

"Almost." She nods as I lean in eagerly. "It's true that he was left in the castle as a prisoner, but the vampire community was already hanging about in Goreway at the time, like they were all over the country, really. A vampire found the count and turned him into a vampire so he could join us. It was him who sort of gathered the community together to enjoy the castle. Ever since, the castle has been our main hot spot in the area. Enchantments around the woods keep us hidden away so no one knows we're here." She hesitates, adding, "Except you, of course. Somehow they didn't work on you."

"*Wow.*" I can't believe how lucky I am to be able to listen to the REAL VAMPIRE HISTORY of Goreway. "That count in the story isn't . . . Count Bloodthirst, is it?"

"No," she chuckles. "Although he'd be complimented to hear the comparison. That count was notorious for being particularly evil. If it was up to that count, vampires would have taken over the world completely. But the Chosen

Leader at the time reminded him that vampires needed humans around."

"Have you heard of a man named Arthur Quince?" I ask, very much not keen to linger on why exactly vampires needed humans around.

She frowns. "Who?"

"He lived in Goreway a long time ago, in the nineteenth century. He was saved from a vampire attack by a mysterious person who appeared by the woods. Do you know this story?"

"No, I don't think so," she says, interested. "But vampires don't really go around talking about times they failed, so maybe that particular vampire didn't want to shout about the incident. How did the person save him?"

"I don't really know," I admit with a sigh, worried that I'll never know the real story of Arthur Quince and his savior. "I thought you might be able to tell me."

"It's unlikely that a person can stop a vampire without, you know"—she leans in to whisper, as though telling me a great secret—"sticking a wooden stake through their heart."

"There's nothing a human can say to keep the vampire at bay?" I ask weakly, knowing it sounds ridiculous.

"No," she confirms, before her expression brightens as

she informs me, "There are other ways to keep us away, though, if you want. Garlic is the big one. Wow, does that smell GROSS. It literally burns our nostrils. Apparently, humans sometimes put it in their food? Bleugh. Oh, and if you want to avoid us, then sunlight is a big help. We won't go near that stuff, as you know."

She hesitates and her face suddenly drops. "You're not looking for ways to avoid me, are you?"

"No! Definitely not," I assure her as her shoulders relax in relief. "I knew all that already, don't worry. I just wanted to know if a story I'd heard was true. You see, I might not be the first human to make contact with the vampire community of Skeleton Woods. I wanted to know if that could be the case."

"Phew. I'm glad we're still *friends* and you're not going to shove a garlic bulb in my mouth or anything," she says brightly.

"I would never do that. You saved my life. I owe you big-time."

"You don't owe me anything, Maggie Helsby," she tells me sternly. "You gave me a human fiction book."

I grin at her. "Right. About that . . ."

"You're not going to take it away, are you?" She gasps, waking up Bat-Ears, who lets out an indignant screech before drifting off into an upside-down doze again. "I haven't read the end yet. I need to know what happens."

"I'm not going to take it away. But I was wondering if you might consider enjoying a bit more of the human world. I thought maybe you might think about venturing out of the woods."

She stares at me. "W-what?"

"You don't have to," I say quickly, trying to read her expression. "But I thought, as you're a vegetarian vampire and you're my friend, you might want to meet my other friends. We could go at nighttime and you'd be able to see a bit more of the world. Not just the castle and these woods. Only if you want, though. There's no pressure."

"I could experience the world that makes things like music and fiction books?"

Her face suddenly convulses, her mouth disappearing and her eyes clamping shut, as though she's just eaten a sour sweet. She lets out a strangled squeak.

"Sharptooth," I say gently, terrified of what's happening, "are you OK?"

She nods and then slowly opens her eyes, looking stunned. "I think . . . I think I was trying to cry! But vampires don't cry! We can't! So it's really quite painful!"

"Oh my goodness, I'm so sorry!" I yelp, horrified that my suggestion caused such a reaction. "Forget I said anything. Forget the whole idea. It's not important."

"Not important?" She shakes her head at me. "Maggie, it's the most *important* idea I've ever had the honor of hearing!"

I blink at her. "It is?"

"Yes. I would *love* to go into the human world where there are friends and music and no one threatening to rip my head off if I spill beet juice on their cloak one more time."

"Well, I can't make any promises," I joke, laughing nervously about the idea of this Maggothead vampire. "But that's great, Sharptooth. Really great."

"How exciting," she says, grinning wonkily, still getting to grips with smiling. "I hope your friends don't smell too good!"

"I hope so, too, Sharptooth," I reply, glancing at her sharp fangs. "I really hope so, too."

*H*ow do you ask your friends if they want to meet a vampire?

I've been panicking about it all day, trying to work out the best way of casually sliding it into conversation. I was staring out the window during my geography lesson, lost in thought about how best to approach the subject, when my teacher suddenly called out, "Maggie Helsby, what did I just say?" in a very stern voice.

"Uh . . ." I glanced down at the page my textbook was open at for help. "Something about Minsk?"

The rest of the class burst into giggles and my cheeks flushed red as the teacher sighed heavily.

"No, Maggie, I was not talking about Minsk," the teacher corrected me crossly. "We did capital cities last week. Today, I've been talking about rivers and erosion. Would you be so kind as to *pay attention?*"

I said that I would, but that's easier said than done when you're trying to work out how to introduce a vampire into your friendship group. I spent the rest of the lesson doing my best to look fascinated by the topic of riverbanks, but my eyes were secretly glazed over as my brain struggled to find the right answer for how to talk to Ari and Miles.

"You know how you said you *weren't* distracted at the moment?" Ari says to me during lunch break, sitting on one of the benches outside by the sports fields. "I want to believe you, Maggie, but you genuinely look worried ALL the time. Is everything OK?"

"Actually, there is something I want to talk to you both about," I begin tentatively.

"Is it to do with how many jokes Ari makes?" Miles asks, his brow furrowed. "I have told her she tells too many."

"Oh please." Ari snorts. "Maggie loves my jokes. If there's anything we need to discuss, it's your negativity, Miles. It wouldn't kill you to be a little more upbeat."

Miles frowns. "That's not—"

"It's absolutely nothing to do with either of you," I announce hurriedly before they can start properly bickering. "It's to do with . . . my friend."

"Which friend?" Ari says, crossing her arms. "Is that code for Miles?"

"No," I assure them.

They watch me expectantly as I shift in my seat, still unsure of what I'm going to say and how best to put it. I start fidgeting with my shirt collar, checking that no one else is nearby, before leaning in and lowering my voice so it's just about audible.

"This is going to sound a bit strange, and you have to promise that what I'm about to say stays a secret between us three. Promise?"

"Promise," they say in unison.

"OK." I take a deep breath. "That day we went to Skeleton Woods, I met someone there. In the woods, I mean. And not just anyone. I . . . uh . . . well, I met a vampire."

They both blink at me.

"What?" Ari says eventually.

"I met a vampire," I repeat. "Her name is Sharptooth Shadow and she's a vegetarian vampire. So don't worry! Nothing to be afraid of. She lives off beet juice. Anyway, we've sort of formed a friendship and I wondered whether you might be interested in meeting her. Tonight, in fact. It has to be the evening because of the whole sunlight-turning-her-to-dust thing. But that's why I've been quite busy lately. I've been meeting her in the woods and learning about her world. In return, I've told her a bit about ours. She's never had a friend before. I thought it would be nice for her to meet you two as well. She's great. You'll really like her."

I come to the end of my reel and wait for a reaction. Miles's jaw is hanging open. Ari is peering at me, her eyes narrowed and suspicious.

"Maggie," she begins slowly, "have you . . . banged your head lately? Maybe fallen off your bike? Because you're kind of not making any sense. You're saying that you met a vampire. And you've been hanging out with her."

"That's right," I confirm. "I have."

"A vampire," Miles says in a low voice, his eyes darting back and forth between me and Ari.

"Yes. I know it sounds strange—"

"Maggie," Ari begins, shaking her head.

"—but it's true!" I insist, cutting her off before she can tell me I've lost my mind. "All those stories about Skeleton Woods, about vampires lurking in there, they're on the right lines. Why would I make this up? What would be the point?"

"To freak out Miles?" Ari suggests.

"You remember the feeling you both got stepping through that mist of Skeleton Woods? Those are enchantments. They keep everyone away from stumbling upon the vampire community that lives there."

"Then how did you find one?" Miles asks curiously.

I falter. "I . . . I don't know. They didn't work on me for some reason. But that's not the point. The point is that Sharptooth is a really good person—"

"Vampire," Ari corrects me, raising her eyebrows.

"Fine, she's a really *good* vampire," I emphasize, desperate for them to believe me. "And I want to help her. You should have seen her face when I played music to her for the first time. It was like seeing someone witness magic or something. I like hanging out with her and I think you would, too. I think she deserves more friends."

Ari and Miles stare at me, both seemingly at a loss for what to say next.

"At least let her hang out with us tonight," I say eventually, interrupting the silence. "That way you can see if I'm making it all up or not."

"But what if you're not making it up?" Miles says, his eyes widening. "Then we'll be meeting a *vampire*."

"She won't hurt you," I remind him.

"I suppose there's no harm in you bringing your . . . uh . . . new friend to hang out with us," Ari says, unconvinced. "I mean, I don't really know what to say, Maggie. It's all a bit . . . nuts."

"I get that. I wasn't sure if I'd made it all up in my head the first time. But it's real."

The bell rings for the start of afternoon lessons and I jump up happily, pleased that it's out in the open and they've agreed to meet Sharptooth.

"I think it's best if we stick around the woods for tonight," I suggest, having already planned this bit in my head. "We don't want to take her too much out of her comfort zone to start with. So, we can go there after school, but I promise I won't make you go into the woods or anything."

"If I'm meeting a vampire tonight, I'll need to stop by a shop on the way to stuff my pockets with garlic bulbs," Miles declares.

"Please don't do that!" I blurt out so passionately that they both look a bit taken aback. "Sorry, but that really is true about vampires hating garlic and I don't want her to be uncomfortable."

"Sure," Ari says, standing up and watching me curiously. "We don't want the *vampire* to feel uncomfortable in the group."

"Like I said, she won't hurt you. She only drinks beet juice. Oh, and you'll meet her bat, too. Every vampire has one, they're like a little sidekick. Hers is called Bat-Ears and he's really sweet, but make sure you act afraid if he jumps out at you when we get there. He's been practicing his evil entrance and I think I dented his confidence a bit yesterday."

They share a look.

"OK, this has been . . . interesting," Miles says, staring warily at me. "But we better get to lessons before we're late."

"Cool, and remember," I add in a whisper as we walk toward the school building, "keep everything I've said a secret. Nobody can know but us."

"Oh, you don't need to worry about that," Ari assures me. "We won't be telling *anyone* about this."

I know they think I've lost my marbles. But soon they'll see that everything I've said is the truth. I just hope nothing goes wrong.

Before I left her yesterday, Sharptooth and I formulated a plan. I would meet her with my friends outside the woods on the path next to the KEEP OUT sign closest to the trees. That way, she was stepping out of the woods and into the open, but was close enough that Bat-Ears could keep watch and signal if something was amiss. It also meant that Ari and Miles wouldn't have to go into the woods again, something I knew neither of them would agree to.

"Can't I come into Goreway?" she asked me eagerly at first when I made the suggestion. "I want to see the town!"

"Not yet," I said. "Small steps first."

She reluctantly agreed.

When school finishes, Ari and Miles come home with me, and after dinner, we ask Mum and Dad if it's all right for us to go for a walk.

"It's getting dark," Mum observes, glancing out the window.

"We won't go far," I say, trying to sound casual. "We just want to try out a new trick on my bike."

They agree that we can go, but we have to be back inside within the hour.

"Not a problem," Miles squeaks, stopping at the door. "We'll be back as soon as possible, Mr. and Mrs. Helsby. In fact, do we really want to go out at all?"

"Come on, Miles," Ari sighs, ushering him out.

I take my bike and helmet to keep up the pretense, walking it along next to me as Ari and Miles trail behind. When I really think about it, I'm lucky that I managed to persuade them to get this far. I feel strangely nervous as I approach the sign where we're meeting.

Am I doing the right thing introducing Sharptooth to Miles and Ari? I think as we come to a stop. *What if they spill the secret accidentally? Or what if they don't get on?*

"What if the vampire eats us?" Miles says aloud.

"Then we'll be dead," Ari answers simply.

Miles gulps. I turn to reassure him for the hundredth time that Sharptooth won't hurt us, while Ari shoves her hands into her pockets, likely wondering why she's bothering to entertain this whole foolish notion. I swivel back to face the woods, resting my bike against the sign. I quickly text my mum to let her know that we're having a fun time on the path "just out of view of the house." It is dark and I don't want them worrying. If I keep messaging my parents, they'll be less likely to come out and call us in. I put my phone away.

Then we wait.

I suddenly see two red dots appear in the darkness and smile. Looking very nervous, Sharptooth shuffles out,

Bat-Ears swooping through the evening air ahead of her. The sun has set now, but that doesn't stop her from anxiously looking up at the sky beyond the safety of the trees.

She lifts her foot, and with her toe pointed she takes a slow, dramatic step out from the woods. Nothing happens. Looking delighted, she takes another step.

She smiles broadly. "YAY! I didn't combust!"

"*Oh. My. God,*" Ari breathes.

"That's not . . . it can't be . . . is that . . ." Miles trails off, his lip quivering.

"Maggie," Ari says, grabbing my arm, her voice a few pitches higher than normal, "is this some kind of trick? Have you paid this person to hide in the woods and come out and scare us? Is this a joke?"

I shake my head. "I promise I'm not playing a trick on you. But it's OK. Like I said, she won't hurt you and you don't need to be afraid."

Sharptooth is closer now, her red eyes wide with anticipation as she stares at Ari and then at Miles. Bat-Ears flutters around her head, as nervous as she is, before landing on her shoulder. Sharptooth quickly brushes down her cloak, making sure there are no creases, and stands up tall as though she's meeting royalty.

"Sharptooth," I begin, clearing my throat, "this is Ari and Miles. They're my friends."

"Hello, Ari and Miles," she says, giving them a wave. "I'm outside the woods."

"Yes, well done," I say encouragingly as she beams at me. "That must have been a bit nerve-racking. And no one saw you?"

"Count Bloodthirst is busy teaching badminton in the dungeons," she assures me, before turning excitedly to Ari and Miles. "That's one of his hobbies, even though he's evil. I know humans have hobbies, too. Do you have hobbies, Ari and Miles?"

I'm not entirely sure either of them are prepared to speak quite yet. Both look frozen to the spot, staring at Sharptooth wide-eyed. Miles looks as though he might faint at any moment.

"Are you . . . are you *really* a vampire?" Ari manages to get out.

"Oh yes." Sharptooth nods proudly. "But as I've told Maggie, I'm a vegetarian, so you have nothing to worry about. And this is Bat-Ears. He's a very evil bat."

"Is this real?" Ari asks in disbelief. "Is this really happening?"

"Yes," I tell her. "Maybe we should all sit down."

I lead by example, sitting down on the grass, while Sharptooth happily follows suit. Once Ari sits, Miles lowers himself very slowly to the ground, his hands shaking, his eyes fixed on Sharptooth as though she might pounce any minute.

Nobody says anything. I rack my brains to think of a topic to start off a conversation, but Sharptooth gets there before me.

"You both smell nice."

Miles looks at her in alarm.

"Thanks," Ari says, glancing nervously at me. "I like your . . . uh . . . cloak."

"Thanks!" Sharptooth replies, ecstatic. "I didn't spill anything on it today. I was extra careful in Dribble Class."

"What's Dribble Class?" Ari asks.

"Well, it's—"

"You know what?" I quickly interrupt, a little too high-pitched. "Ari is an amazing artist, Sharptooth. Do vampires draw? Ari, you should show her some of your illustrations."

"We have paintings in the castle," Sharptooth tells Ari enthusiastically. "But I think they were done by humans a long time ago. Vampires aren't supposed to do any kind of art. According to vampire rules, anything enjoyable like that is pointless and we're better off spending our time learning how to dodge wooden stakes."

"Oh," Ari says as Sharptooth continues to smile wonkily at her. "I guess . . . I guess that is handy. Dodging wooden stakes."

"Yes. If we don't dodge them, we die," Sharptooth says jovially.

"Right. That can't be fun. But . . . um . . ."

Ari hesitates, glancing at me. I smile at her encouragingly. She reaches into her schoolbag and pulls out her book that's crammed with loose drawings. She selects one and passes it over to Sharptooth, who takes it, examining the sketched dragon closely.

"This is some of the art I've done," Ari explains, gesturing to the drawing in Sharptooth's lap. "Respectfully to the vampire rules, art definitely isn't a waste of time. At least, not in my opinion anyway."

Sharptooth stares at the picture in amazement. "It's *beautiful*. Did you make this?"

"Yeah. I've done these as well." She hands over some more of her drawings, Sharptooth taking them in her hands as carefully as if they were made of glass.

"I've never seen anything like this," Sharptooth whispers, carefully admiring each drawing, one by one. "You are a very, very talented human, Ari."

Ari can't help but smile at Sharptooth's enamored expression as she traces the drawings with a sharp, pointed fingernail. "Thanks. I'm glad you like them. If you want, I can give you some paper and sketching pencils, and you can give it a try yourself."

Sharptooth blinks at her. "You think . . . you think *I* might be able to draw like this?"

"Sure," Ari says, tearing out some paper from her pad and selecting a couple of pencils from a case in her bag. "Why not? Give it a try. Hopefully, you'll enjoy it."

"Wow." Sharptooth takes the paper and pens, slipping them into a pocket inside her cloak, before turning to me. "First you give me a fiction book, now I get to do some drawings. I'm so glad I met you, Maggie."

I laugh, glancing at Miles to check he's OK. He hasn't said anything in a while and I'm not surprised to find him still sitting tensely with his eyes locked on Sharptooth, his brain no doubt whirring through how this defies logic and wondering how to possibly handle the situation.

"Sharptooth, did I tell you that Miles is really good at

sports?" I say. "He's on all the teams at school. Miles, Sharptooth is crazy fast and super strong. Is there any chance you can show him how fast you are, Sharptooth?"

"If I run as fast as I can with him, his legs will definitely snap and he may die," Sharptooth replies matter-of-factly, which is extremely unhelpful.

"Right, but maybe, instead, you could just run around, so we can *witness* how fast you are. Rather than experience it."

"OK!"

She jumps to her feet. Her sudden movement makes Miles flinch, but he collects himself on noticing Ari's grin. Sharptooth swishes her cloak behind her—with the smallest of stumbles; she's honestly come a long way in that department—and disappears in a blur. As she whooshes past, Miles gasps, clutching his heart, before in a matter of seconds she's at our side again.

I'm pretty sure the realistic getup and the live bat on her shoulder was enough of a confirmation, but if they didn't believe Sharptooth was a vampire before, they do now.

"Whoa," Ari says, grinning from ear to ear.

"That was six miles," she tells us, plonking back down onto the grass. "I went back into the woods and ran there. I didn't want to run too far out."

"Very sensible," I say, before looking to Miles. "What do you think?"

Shell-shocked at first, slowly the corners of his mouth twitch into a smile.

"I think," he begins, beaming at the vampire sitting across the way from him, "that was AWESOME."

I t turns out playing sports with a vampire is a bit of a depressing affair.

"OK, Sharptooth," Miles begins, taking a soccer ball out of his bag and rolling it onto the ground. "The aim of this game is to score by kicking the ball into the net." He points to where he's put a couple of our schoolbags standing in for goalposts a few feet away. "Or for now, as we don't have a net, in between those two bags."

"Sounds simple enough," Sharptooth says enthusiastically, clapping her hands. "Nowhere near as complicated as badminton. No wonder vampires don't bother with soccer."

"Actually, it's not as simple as it sounds," Miles says, trying not to look offended. "When it's played properly, you have two teams so you come against defenders who will be trying their best to stop you."

"Oooh! Do they stop you by trying to kill you?"

Miles grimaces. "No. They just . . . tackle you."

"Oh." Sharptooth shrugs. "Not overly exciting, then."

Ari and I try to stifle our laughter, while Miles looks furious, pretending to sort out his headlamp so Sharptooth doesn't notice his thunderous expression.

This isn't the first time Sharptooth has ruined sports for Miles. Since their first meeting, Ari and Miles have come with me twice to see Sharptooth, and last time Miles attempted to introduce Sharptooth to cricket. When it was her time to bat, she hit the ball so far out, it was lost forever, and then did about five hundred runs at lightning speed before we yelled at her to stop. Her fielding ability was even more hilarious—she caught every single ball, even when Miles tried to get away with tapping it so lightly it plopped just in front of him. We blinked and Sharptooth was lying on the ground at his feet yawning, the cricket ball safely in the palm of her hand before it had even bounced.

Since we have to meet her at dusk every time, I think it's almost a good thing that the games finish so quickly. It wouldn't be ideal if they dragged on, as we never have as much time with her as we'd like. She has to time our meetings carefully to make sure there's no chance a vampire might be strolling in the woods and see us in the field beyond. She also has to be sure that she won't be missed for too long and that Count Bloodthirst is preferably teaching a noisy class or down in the dungeons where the walls are thickest—apparently his hearing is so good that that he might hear us at the edge of the woods if we were being too loud.

And *we* need to make sure we don't stay out in the dark so long that my parents will start to worry. As far as they're aware, we're all REALLY into learning new bike tricks at the moment.

I just hope they don't ask me to show them a trick I've been working on any time soon.

Ari and Miles are as in awe of Sharptooth as I am. They can't believe that vampires exist and we get to hang out with one. After the first evening they spent with Sharptooth, they both messaged on our WhatsApp group about a hundred times gushing about what had just happened and wondering if it was real. The next day at school, Ari yelled my name as soon as I got out of the car, came running over, and went, "I didn't dream it, right? Tell me I didn't dream it."

I assured her that she didn't. She looked happier than I've ever seen her.

While Miles was thrilled to be able to introduce Sharptooth to sports, Ari was determined to show her more about the arts. She got busy compiling the perfect playlist of music through the ages, trying to capture the best songs of each decade and of all types of genres. We sat Sharptooth down and, as Ari got the playlist up on her phone, Sharptooth asked what the *phone* was.

That set off a whole new conversation as Ari and Miles attempted to teach Sharptooth how to work a phone. I couldn't stop laughing, as every time the screen changed, Sharptooth would yelp and go, "It's WITCHCRAFT!" She was desperate to touch all the buttons appearing on the screen, so Ari let her type in the notes app before she switched apps to show her something else.

"WHERE DID ALL THE LETTERS GO?" Sharptooth yelled, freaking out.

As Miles pointed out, it's a little like teaching an alien who is visiting Earth for the first time. Everything we take for granted is *amazing* to her. In return, she's been telling us about vampire lessons and making us laugh with impressions of Count Bloodthirst. I've noticed that she hasn't told

Ari and Miles about the whole Chosen Leader thing, so I'm guessing she doesn't want them to know. Maybe she's embarrassed about it. She can tell them when she's ready. I haven't said a word to them about it, feeling honored that she told me.

Speaking of which, I know this sounds a bit odd, but Sharptooth and I seem to have a . . . connection or something. For example, I can always spot her in the woods long before the other two can. I can see her eyes from far away, shining through the darkness, but they can never see her until she's really close.

And I would never say this out loud because it makes me sound like I've lost my mind, but it's as though I can *sense* her, too. Sometimes I know she's near, even though I can't see her eyes quite yet.

It's strange.

"Shall we get playing before it gets too dark for you humans to see?" Sharptooth suggests, gesturing to the soccer ball as Miles finishes straightening up his headlamp.

"Good plan."

"Which way round are we playing?" she asks keenly. "Am I kicking it through the posts and you three defending, or are you kicking it while I defend the goal?"

"Let's start with you trying to score," Miles decides. "Now, you can only kick the ball, you can't touch it with your hands, OK? So you're just dribbling it."

"Dribbling?" She looks confused. "Do I pierce it with my teeth?"

I burst out laughing at the idea of Sharptooth running around a soccer field with the ball stuck to her fangs. "Not that kind of dribbling, Sharptooth. Dribbling the ball is what we call maneuvering and kicking the ball whilst on the move, if that makes sense. You sort of kick it along as you run."

"Want me to show you?" Miles offers.

"No need," Sharptooth says confidently. "I think I can get the hang of it."

I steal a glance at Ari and we both smirk, already knowing what's about to happen. No sooner has Miles yelled "GO!" than Sharptooth is already jumping around in celebration at having dribbled the ball past all three of us and kicked it through the goal. Miles groans, putting his head in his hands.

"I didn't even see the ball move," he sighs, deflated, his arms dropping to his sides. "You know, if we could somehow get Sharptooth on the school team, we'd be undefeated."

"Slightly unfair to the other schools, though," I point

out, grinning at him. "There's got to be something in the rules that says no vampires allowed."

"I wish I could see your school," Sharptooth yells from over by the goal. "Do you think I can come into Goreway with you soon?"

"It's very risky, Sharptooth," I reply anxiously, Miles and Ari nodding. "What if someone sees you and works out who you really are?"

She walks over wearing a downcast expression. "If only I could blend in somehow."

"You're not missing much," Miles offers, checking the time on his phone as it starts to get darker. "It's not the biggest of towns."

"If it makes you feel any better, I wish we could see the castle," Ari says wistfully. "It sounds amazing. But I guess we'll never get to see it."

"It's lucky that Maggie got out alive," Sharptooth reminds her before her face lights up. "I could draw it for you maybe! With my paper and pencils! Then you can sort of see what it's like. Although drawing is very hard. I tried to draw Bat-Ears the other night and it came out looking like a blob with ears."

"Hey, speaking of drawing, I have one for you," Ari

laughs, remembering something and running to grab her bag now that it's no longer needed as a goalpost.

She rummages about in it before pulling out an illustration of Sharptooth. She's been working on it for the past couple of days, making sure she got the details just right. She hands the drawing over to Sharptooth.

"A vampire!" Sharptooth exclaims. "That's cool. I like their hair."

"It's not just any vampire," I say quickly, glancing at Ari, who looks disappointed by the reaction. "Don't you see who it is?"

Sharptooth looks at us blankly. "Who? I didn't realize you knew any other vampires!"

"It's . . . it's you, Sharptooth," Ari says quietly. "Sorry, maybe it's not a very good likeness. My style is to do it like this, you know, illustrations, rather than serious portraits. But you don't have to keep it or anything to be polite. I just thought—"

Sharptooth gasps, holding it up and pointing at the figure. "This is ME?"

"Yes! It's really good," Miles insists as Ari shifts from one foot to the other, looking at the ground in embarrassment. "It looks exactly like you!"

"WOW! This is AMAZING!" Sharptooth cries, hugging it to her and then holding it out again. "Is this really what I look like? I look FABULOUS!"

"Hang on a minute." I stare at her in disbelief as the truth dawns on me. "Vampires can't see their reflections!"

"No," Sharptooth confirms, studying the picture closely. "I've never seen my reflection before."

"Of course!" Ari says, looking relieved. "That whole myth about vampires avoiding mirrors because they have no reflection! I didn't even THINK about that."

"Guess it's not a myth after all," Miles laughs. "So this drawing is the first time you've ever seen what you look like?"

Sharptooth nods, admiring it still. "It's so strange to see myself. It must be accurate because you've got Bat-Ears just right." She chuckles, pointing to the drawing of him flying above her head, his outrageously fluffy belly on display, his eyes narrowed in determination. "He has this exact expression whenever he's grumpy."

Bat-Ears, sitting on her shoulder and also peering at the illustration, screeches in protest.

Something about this conversation bugs me and I have no idea why. Like there's a niggle in the back of my brain, something I'm trying to remember, but I can't.

"We should get home," Miles prompts. "It's getting really dark and your parents will be wondering where we are, Maggie."

"Yeah, sorry, Sharptooth," I say, going to pick up my bag. "I wish we could have longer."

"Don't worry, I need to get back for meditation time anyway," she reveals. "Thanks so much for my drawing and for teaching me soccer! It was lots of fun."

"For you," Miles adds grumpily under his breath.

"Vampires meditate?" Ari asks with interest. "That seems . . . unlikely."

"It's very good for us. We lie in our coffins and close our eyes and, you know, focus on ourselves, connecting with our inner world."

"Who knew vampires were so deep?" Ari says, lifting her eyebrows in surprise. "No offense, Sharptooth."

"None taken," Sharptooth replies cheerily. "I know vampires aren't really renowned for great thinking. Probably because everyone gets distracted by how good we are at cloak swishing."

"Yeah," Miles says, sharing a smile with Ari. "Cloak swishing is what vampires are known for."

We say our goodbyes, arrange our next meetup at the

weekend, and then, as Sharptooth disappears into the woods, the rest of us head back to my house where Mum is waiting to give Ari and Miles a lift home.

Having said goodbye, I'm wandering across the landing toward my bedroom when it suddenly hits me. The niggle at the back of my head, the thing I couldn't put my finger on earlier. I stop still on the landing and glance from one bedroom to another, each one with its door wide open.

Vampires don't have reflections.

It was one of the first things I noticed about this house when we moved in. One of the first things I thought was strange about the way Great-Uncle Bram lived. I spin around and race back down the stairs to the living room where Dad is sitting on the sofa with a book. He glances up from it as I barge in through the door.

"You all right, Maggie?"

"Dad, can I ask you a question about Great-Uncle Bram?"

"You can, although I'm not sure I'll be able to answer," he chuckles. "I barely knew him."

"Why did he put huge mirrors up in every room?"

Dad blinks at me, confused. "What?"

"Haven't you noticed? In every single room of the house, in every corridor or hallway even, there is a giant mirror." I gesture to the striking and heavy gold-framed mirror above the mantelpiece opposite us as an example.

"Is it strange to have mirrors in the house?" He frowns, reaching for his bookmark to save his page before closing the book. "I haven't really thought about it, other than that it would be a hassle to take them all down. Might as well use them since they're already up."

"But, Dad"—I move to sit down on the sofa next to him—"they're everywhere. Who has a big mirror in the kitchen? And up the stairs? Don't you think that's unusual? It's almost as if he . . ."

When I trail off, Dad prompts me. "Almost as if he what? Liked to check on his appearance?"

Almost as if he wanted to make sure that anyone who entered his house had a reflection.

"Never mind," I say, slumping back onto the cushions, rubbing my forehead as it starts to ache and whispering to myself, "That and the garlic around the house."

"What about it?" Dad laughs. "I told you, he must have enjoyed the soup. Home-grown vegetables are delicious!"

I let out a long, drawn-out sigh. "Do you know *anything* about Great-Uncle Bram at all? What he did for a job? Who he spent time with?"

"He was a simple man who kept to himself." Dad shrugs. "Not interested in much, no hobbies, no friends. A harmless, rather clueless gentleman, from what I've heard."

"And you're *sure* that you don't know anything about us being related to Mina Helsby, the author?" I ask, a question that I've already pestered him with before.

"Like I told you when you first got that book from the library, I've never heard of her. It would have been cool to be related to a Goreway historian from so long ago, but I think it's just a coincidence that we share the same surname. It happens."

I bite my lip, deep in thought.

"Maggie?" Dad taps me on the shoulder, an expression of concern on his face. "Is there something bothering you? You look . . . confused."

For a moment, I consider telling him some of the questions buzzing through my brain, but I don't want to give away anything to do with Skeleton Woods and Sharptooth.

"Nothing," I assure him, attempting a relaxed smile. "I just thought the mirrors were a bit odd, but I guess you're right. Not that strange at all, now that I think about it. I'm going to go upstairs and do some reading. See you in a bit."

I push myself up from the sofa and can feel him

watching me as I leave. When I get upstairs, I stop at Mum and Dad's room, what was Great-Uncle Bram's. Checking that Dad hasn't followed me up, I quietly tiptoe in and look around for any clues, anything that could be connected to Bram, perhaps something left behind. Seeing just my parents' things dotted about everywhere, I shake my head. I'm being stupid. All his things would have been cleared out when he passed away.

I'm about to head out of the room when I catch my reflection in the gigantic mirror hanging on the wall, framed exactly the same as the one downstairs and the one in my bedroom. That intricate, chunky gold frame that makes the mirror jut out from the wall slightly.

I wonder . . .

I creep toward it and, glancing over my shoulder to make sure I'm definitely alone, I reach around behind the mirror and feel for anything there. I run my hand down the back from the middle of the frame, which is as high as I can reach. Suddenly, my hand hits an object tucked away, right at the bottom. My breath catching in my throat, I wrap my fingers around it and carefully pull it out. My whole body goes cold as I hold it up in front of me.

Sitting in the palms of my hands is a very sharp wooden stake.

It looks like what Dad heard about Great-Uncle Bram was wrong. He wasn't clueless.

He wasn't clueless at all.

13

I have had an amazing idea," Ari announces proudly, looping her arm through mine as we walk toward the school one morning. "I am a GENIUS."

"I'm not sure you're allowed to declare yourself a genius," Miles says, falling into step with us. "We'll be the judge of that, once we've heard the idea."

"All right then, prepare to worship me."

She makes us stop before we reach the school steps, looking around to check no one is nearby, and then leaning in conspiratorially.

"Halloween," she says simply, a wide grin spreading across her face.

"What about it?" Miles asks.

"It's this week."

"And?"

"And what better night *to sneak a vampire into town*?!"

157

Miles frowns. "You mean . . ."

"I mean, everyone is going to be dressed up as spooky characters!" she whispers, barely able to contain her excitement. "Sharptooth will fit right in!"

I grab Ari's arm, wondering why I hadn't thought of it before. "That is BRILLIANT!"

"I KNOW!" Ari cries, before shooting Miles a smug smile. "Aren't I a genius? Come on, you can admit it now."

"I guess it might work," he says thoughtfully. "There's still a lot of risk."

"There's barely any risk!" Ari protests. "Look, this may be her only opportunity to come see our world like she's always wanted. The one night of the year where someone who looks like a vampire won't stand out, they'll blend in. No one will look twice at her. It's GENIUS."

"It really is, Ari!" I exclaim, beaming at her. "We can dress up as vampires, too. No one will question it."

"What about your parents?" Miles says, nudging me with his elbow. "Have you forgotten their big Halloween plans?"

I realize Miles has a point. My parents asked if they could host a Halloween dinner this year with Ari and Miles as our guests of honor before taking us into town to go trick-or-treating. Unsurprisingly, Dad has always been BIG on Halloween, insisting that we celebrate all things spooky, and I love it. We usually have a delicious spooky-themed feast before watching scary movies, all three of us in costume. I never do trick-or-treating because, before, I was too embarrassed to either go on my own or, my only other option, go with my parents. But this year, Dad has been very enthusiastic about making a big night of it with my new friends.

"I don't see why that's an issue," Ari tells Miles stubbornly. "Sharptooth can join us for dinner at Maggie's. She'll love it!"

Miles looks at her as if she's got three eyes. "You think we can invite Sharptooth to sit at a dining table with Maggie's parents and act normally? What exactly do you expect her to eat, Ari?"

"Well, I don't know about you, but I think it's a good idea for Sharptooth to branch out in terms of her taste buds. She must be getting bored of beet juice. She can try new stuff!"

"What about all the big mirrors in the house?" Miles says, folding his arms. "There are too many obstacles."

Ari frowns, trying to work out how to argue back, but

Miles is right. Our house is designed to keep vampires out. I know now that Great-Uncle Bram specifically made it that way. He was always prepared for an attack. I suppose I'll never find out if he simply *believed* all the stories that drove him through the roof, or whether he *knew* that vampires weren't very far away.

But if he knew for sure, why would he stay in Skeleton Lodge?

Ari suddenly clicks her fingers, snapping me out of my thoughts.

"I've got it. Let's propose to your parents that we have an outdoor meal! Your dad loves all this spooky stuff, right? So let's come up with a plan he can't refuse! We can have a campfire, tell one another scary stories. He'll love it! That way Sharptooth can join us and we don't have to worry about her going in the house. There you go, Miles, I've done it. I've worked out the perfect plan. And do you know why? Because I'm a GENIUS."

Ari starts dancing on the spot and Miles and I can't help but laugh.

"I guess that *might* work," Miles says, shaking his head at Ari as she bops her shoulders. "What do you think, Maggie?"

"I think it's worth a try." I high-five Ari, who lets out a triumphant squeal. "Inviting a vampire for dinner with my parents. What could go wrong?"

My parents' reaction to my Halloween costume couldn't be better.

It's not exactly the most imaginative look, but clearly they were expecting something else, because I enter the kitchen, give one swish of my cloak standing in the doorway, and Mum yelps, dropping the pan she was holding. It clatters loudly on the floor. Luckily, she hadn't put any food in it yet.

"I'll take that as proof that I look scary enough for Halloween," I laugh, giving her and Dad a full spin. "What do you think?"

Miles, Ari, and I all ordered identical cloaks, complete with the high collar, and the most realistic fake fangs we could find online. Ari had messaged a series of links to YouTube tutorials that helped with the makeup side of things, and we'd even gone so far as to order contact lenses that turned our eyes red and matching silver-haired wigs.

When I added the rubber bat, hanging from invisible string tied to my sleeve, I stared at my reflection in the mirror and was elated at how similar I looked to Sharptooth. I felt proud to match her.

"My goodness, you gave me a fright," Mum says, picking up the pan and glancing to Dad. "You look great. Like a real-life vampire standing in our doorway! For a moment, I thought—"

"Yes," Dad jumps in, dressed as Captain Hook and busily arranging cupcakes on a tray, spiders and webs iced all over the top of them. "Very lifelike! I'm impressed at all the detail! What made you decide on a vampire?"

"Nothing specific," I lie, moving to admire the cupcakes and hopefully steal one. "The four of us decided we'd all go as the same thing. I didn't have much say in it."

"We're very excited to meet this other friend of yours," Mum says, smiling at me. "What was her name again?"

"Shar," I remind them.

When I first asked if another friend from school could join our Halloween plans, they asked me her name and I started saying "Shar—" before I could stop myself. I had to go with it.

"I hope she likes cupcakes. I got overexcited and baked way too many," Dad admits.

"I told you that she's eaten already," I say quickly. "She'll probably be too full to have anything. Is everything set up outside?"

"Oh yes." Dad nods, his chest puffing out proudly. "Want to come with me to start up the campfire and wait for the others to arrive?"

Dad and I head out into the cold night air to the end of the backyard, where we've created the perfect setting for a Halloween party, away from the front bit with all the garlic, as I specifically requested. Dad LOVED the idea of hosting the Halloween dinner outside when I suggested it, persuading Mum that the darkness would add to the atmosphere. I spent the afternoon helping him put fairy lights up everywhere, and we've put down various picnic blankets and rugs covered in colorful cushions, all circled around a small log campfire in the middle. We added a finishing touch of pumpkins and candles dotted about the blankets along with fake spiders and spiderwebs.

As Dad sorts out the campfire, I nervously glance around the yard, my eyes searching just beyond the fence. Sharptooth is out there somewhere, lying in wait. We decided that she would make her entrance at the same time as Ari and Miles, so that she'd have as much support in this daunting scenario as possible.

When the car headlights appear in the distance, signaling the imminent arrival of Miles and Ari, I inhale sharply in anticipation. Ari's dad pulls up and parks at the gate and Dad strolls over to chat to him through the car window, while Miles and Ari jump out of the back seat and come running down the path. They both look brilliant in their vampire costumes and we huddle together.

"When do you think Sharptooth will get here?" Ari asks breathlessly.

"Could be any moment."

"I can't believe we're doing this," Miles squeaks. "I'm really excited and nervous at the same time!"

"Me too." I nod.

"Me too," Ari agrees.

"Me too," Sharptooth says.

"ARGH!"

The three of us jump out of our skin. Sharptooth is right there next to us, looking surprised at our shocked reaction.

"How do you *do* that?" Miles asks, clutching his heart. "Creep up without making a sound."

"Because I'm a vampire," Sharptooth whispers, her brow furrowed in confusion that he hasn't caught on to it yet.

Miles rolls his eyes and tells her firmly he *knows* that. "Where's Bat-Ears?"

"Here." She carefully pulls open her cloak to reveal Bat-Ears fast asleep, hanging from the inside lining. "He's quite happy to stay hidden all evening. He doesn't really like the cold. You all look *amazing*. You should dress like this all the time! It's a shame you all smell so much, otherwise you'd blend right in at the castle!"

"How are you feeling about being so far from the woods?" I ask her quickly, as Ari and Miles share a look of confusion over the smell comment. I notice Miles take a quick sniff under his arm when no one's looking.

"I feel good." She nods before glancing up at the house. "Although there's something about this place. I can't put my finger on it, but my warning senses are tingling."

"Warning senses?"

"When you get a feeling that you shouldn't be somewhere," she explains. "You know it's wrong or the risk is high, but you're doing it anyway. Do humans get that, too?"

Miles nods, letting out a long sigh as he gives Ari a pointed look. "All the time."

"That's just being out of the woods, though, surely," I reason. "It's not to do with Skeleton Lodge in particular, right?"

"I'm not sure," she says, her eyes darting warily around the outside of the house. "My senses felt out of control as I approached the house. I backed away from it earlier and felt fine. As soon as I crept toward it again, the feeling returned. It's probably nothing."

"Ah, Shar has arrived, I see!" Dad calls out, approaching us, having said goodbye to Ari's dad. "Nice to meet you! I'm Maggie's dad."

He does his classic Captain Hook dad joke that he's done several times with me since changing into his costume, where he holds out a hook instead of his hand and bursts out laughing as though it's completely original. Sharptooth looks thrown. Luckily, he's laughing too hard at his own joke to notice her confused expression, and, still chuckling, holds out his other hand for her to shake.

"Goodness, your hands are like ice!" Dad comments as Sharptooth quickly pulls her hand away, tucking it under her cloak. "When did you get here? I didn't see you arrive!"

"My human parents dropped me off at your house in their vehicle," Sharptooth says robotically, as though she's memorized it. "Because that's how we get around."

"Oh, did they? I didn't spot them!" Dad exclaims, putting his hand and hook on his hips. "Clearly, I was too distracted telling Ari's dad all about the new dental practice. We just got a brand-new X-ray machine, state-of-the-art stuff. So if you kids get any pain in those fangs of yours," he adds, chortling, "you let me know!"

"These are not real fangs," Sharptooth cries out in a panic, covering her mouth with her hand. "Right, Maggie? Tell him!"

"Ha ha, very funny, Shar," I say, nervously laughing and thumping her on the back. "But we're all in character tonight. These are totally REAL fangs, Dad, so you better watch out!"

"I sure will!" Dad says, beaming at us. "Now, you vampires go sit down and start the scary stories around the fire and we'll bring the food out in just a moment. And remember"—he puts on a low, scary voice—"beware the evil spirits that lurk in the darkness, the ghosts and ghouls who haunt the fields, the witches whose yellow eyes watch you from a distance, cackling over their cauldrons, and the monsters who can POUNCE!"

He grabs Miles's shoulders, making Miles yelp in fear, before saying "Gotcha!" and wandering into the house, chuckling away.

"Your dad really loves Halloween," Ari notes, smiling at

his back as he disappears into the house. "I guess a love of the spooky runs in the family."

"Witches don't have yellow eyes," Sharptooth comments matter-of-factly. "They have normal eyes. That's how they blend in with the humans."

"W-witches exist?" Miles asks.

"Are you serious, Miles? You're *literally* friends with a vampire." Ari laughs. "Witches can't come as a shocker for you."

"I was hoping that vampires were the only thing I had to be afraid of," he gulps.

Sharptooth pats his shoulder comfortingly. "I wouldn't worry too much about witches. Their main enemy is warlocks. Witches respect humans, that's why they live amongst you. They only cast spells if you annoy them personally. If you're going to be scared of something other than vampires, I'd be concerned about ghosts. They're creepy."

"A vampire calling ghosts creepy," Miles croaks. "That makes me feel better."

"Is anyone going to comment on the fact that my dad had NO IDEA Sharptooth was a vampire?" I whisper excitedly. "Our plan is working!"

"That's true," Sharptooth says, nodding. "Does this mean I get to go into town with you all?"

"It's looking likely," I tell her happily. "Come on, let's go sit down and tell scary stories to freak each other out."

I lead them over to our Halloween setup and, after admiring it, they each take a seat on the rugs and cushions. I offer blankets around, but we all admit that the heavy cloaks are very handy in keeping us warm. I have a warm fuzzy feeling as I look at everyone around the fire, the light from the flames flickering on their faces. I've never shared the excitement of Halloween with anyone but my parents before, and here I am with two proper friends and a vampire.

I'm not sure you can get much better than that.

After a while, Mum comes out with a plate of food and we all sit up straight, eager to chow down, except for Sharptooth, of course. She has brought her own carton of beet juice, sticking to the pretense that she already ate.

As Mum starts handing around the dish, I notice that Sharptooth stiffens, her eyes widening to saucers, her lips pursing until they disappear behind her fangs.

"Uh, Mum?" I say loudly. "What have you got there?"

"Garlic bread, using the fresh garlic from our garden,"

she announces brightly, shoving the plate right under Sharptooth's nose. "Would you like one, Shar? Help yourself!"

At one whiff, Sharptooth keels over backward.

I scramble to my feet and go to help her, while Mum looks stunned, not sure what's happening.

"My goodness," Mum gasps as I help Sharptooth sit back up, "are you all right?"

"GOOD ONE, SHAR! HA HA," I bellow, patting Sharptooth on the back. "She is SO in character right now! You can't give vampires *garlic*, Mum!"

"Oh! Ooooooh," Mum says, relaxing into a smile and starting to giggle. "Very funny! Of course, no garlic for you vampires. Shar, that was very quick-thinking of you! Are you in the drama society at school?"

"Yes, she's brilliant," Ari jumps in. "Mrs. Helsby, I'll have a garlic bread. Why don't you bring them this way, away from . . . uh . . . over there. They look delicious! Fresh garlic from the garden, you say?"

Mum goes to the other side of the circle to tell Ari all about the garlic bread, while I make sure that Sharptooth is all right.

"Sorry about that," Sharptooth whispers, reaching for

her beet juice and taking a sip. "Had a moment there where I almost died, but I'm OK now."

"*I'm* sorry," I reply, biting my lip, forgetting that I'm wearing fangs. "I should have told Mum and Dad not to cook with any garlic today! I was so worried about everything else, I forgot about that."

"Don't worry, it's good for me to get used to it if I'm going to see a bit more of the human world," Sharptooth insists. "It was a small blip. Everything is just fine now."

I smile at her and move back to my cushion, grateful that Ari has swiped all the garlic bread onto her plate. Dad emerges from the house carrying another tray.

"All right, kids," he says, holding the tray aloft proudly, "who wants some garlic chicken?"

We hear a small, strangled *"Eep"* from Sharptooth and glance over just in time to see her topple backward again.

It's going to be a long night.

No one noticed. Not ONE person noticed that there was a vampire in their midst.

Halloween was a HUGE success and Sharptooth couldn't have been happier. Her smile has become much less wonky now that she's doing it more often, and she was grinning away all night, her fangs fully on show for everyone to see, as we went into town and joined the other trick-or-treaters.

She marveled at absolutely *everything*. She was completely mesmerized by the traffic lights and I think if we'd let her, she would have stood in front of them all night watching them change color. She waved at everyone who passed, shouting "Hello, fellow human!" at them, and remarked on the costume of anyone dressed as a vampire: "You look GREAT! The collar on that cloak is a bit old-fashioned, but the rest of your outfit is SPOT-ON! I love your hair, too.

Gone for the slicked-back look, I see. Vampires aren't so attached to hair gel these days, but I think we should bring it back into fashion!"

The biggest success of the night, though, was . . . ketchup.

Having finished her beet juice and avoided anything to do with garlic as well as she could during our Halloween picnic at the house, she looked interested when I squeezed ketchup on my plate for some fries.

"What's that?" she asked, sniffing curiously. "It smells . . . *good.*"

"It's ketchup. You want to try it?" I held out my plate for her.

She very cautiously dipped her finger in the red sauce and licked it. Her eyes glistened with excitement, a stunned smile spreading across her face.

"What is this magical food?" she whispered in awe.

When my parents weren't looking, I got a spare plate and poured ketchup all over it for her. She finished the whole thing in less than a second. In the end, I just gave her the bottle.

"How did we run out of ketchup?" Mum asked the next day, hunting through the cupboards. "I only just bought a new one!"

Sharptooth is so grateful that I've added a new product to her diet, she won't stop going on about it. Ari and Miles both brought ketchup from their homes to give her today, but we've agreed to use our pocket money to buy her some more soon. The way she consumes it, these bottles won't last long.

"You are the BEST, thank you," she says, clutching the ketchup bottles to her before carefully sliding them into the pockets of her cloak. "Ketchup is my new favorite food! And the best thing is, it looks like blood! Who wouldn't want that?"

"True," I laugh, sitting down next to her and pulling my hat over my ears. "How have you been since Halloween?"

"Count Bloodthirst thinks I'm losing focus," she tells us as Bat-Ears flies over to Ari to get a belly tickle. "He can tell I'm distracted. He found a fiction book in my room and got very cross at me. He asked me where I got it."

"What did you say?" Miles asks, full of concern.

"I said I found it in the woods. He said that no one goes walking in the woods because of the enchantments. So I had to make up a plausible story about a bird stealing the book and then dropping it. I'm not sure he believed me, to be honest."

"You have to be more careful, Sharptooth," I warn her. "We don't want you getting in trouble with Count Blood-thirst. He doesn't sound like the . . . nicest of vampires."

Sharptooth hesitates. "He asked about your house, Maggie."

"What?"

"It was strange," she says, fiddling with the end of her cloak. "He asked me where *exactly* I'd found the book and whether it was in the direction of Skeleton Lodge. When I said I wasn't sure and asked what that had to do with anything, he replied that it must have come from there. That there was no other explanation. Then, when I reminded him what he'd JUST said about the enchantments, he got this weird look on his face, snapped at me, and left the room."

"How weird. What do you think that means?" Ari says, too enraptured to bother tickling Bat-Ears's belly any more. He grumpily returns to his vampire.

"I'm not sure." Sharptooth shrugs before her eyes flicker to me and then back at the ground nervously. "But I do know that . . . well . . ."

"What is it?" I prompt, swallowing the lump in my throat.

"I just can't understand my warning senses," she explains, looking cross at herself for being confused. "They were going berserk when I was around your house, Maggie, but then in the town, nothing. Something about that house . . . it made me feel uneasy. Like I was in danger."

Miles frowns. "I don't understand. You mean, you were *scared* of Maggie's house? But not the rest of Goreway?"

Sharptooth nods.

"But vampires aren't scared of humans or their houses," Ari comments, to which Sharptooth readily agrees.

"Except the mystery man who saved Arthur Quince," I murmur under my breath.

"What did you say, Maggie?"

"Nothing," I say hurriedly. "I was just thinking out loud."

I don't want to go into the story of Arthur Quince now. Partly because it's so long and also because I'm not sure it's relevant. What would be the point in telling them? It happened so long ago and it might be completely made up. I haven't been able to find out anything more about it anyway.

"Don't worry, Maggie. Skeleton Lodge, I'm sure, is perfectly safe," Sharptooth says determinedly, looking right in my eyes.

"I know. I'm fine. I'm sure it's nothing. Count Bloodthirst

probably said the book might come from there because it's the closest house to the woods and there's nowhere else for miles. It's just common sense."

"Exactly. Anyway," Sharptooth says brightly, ready to change the subject, clapping her hands together and disturbing Bat-Ears, who was dozing off in her lap as ever, "let's do something fun. We don't have long and it's cold out. Humans feel the cold, don't they? I don't want my friends to turn into ice blocks. That wouldn't be very nice."

"I have a new game that I thought might be fun," Miles announces, pulling a glow-in-the-dark Frisbee out of his backpack. "What do you think of this, Sharptooth? Ready to catch?"

Ari and I watch as Miles gets up, ready to throw it. I'm grateful not to linger on the conversation about Count Bloodthirst and his interest in Skeleton Lodge.

As Miles sends the Frisbee soaring, Sharptooth watches it fly away in wonder before eagerly leaping to her feet, chasing it. She jumps so high in the air, it looks like she's flying, and lands elegantly, clutching the Frisbee in her hands before hurrying back to us.

"Wow, that was amazing," Miles laughs as Sharptooth hands it back to him.

"That was nothing. Try throwing it higher," she brags.

He throws the Frisbee with as much gusto as he can and we all cheer her on as she zooms off, leaping high up into the air, as if in slow motion, her cloak billowing in the wind and her fangs glistening in the moonlight as Bat-Ears swoops along next to her. Her fingers clutch the Frisbee before she lands with a gentle thud on her feet, swaggering back to our whoops and applause.

"Who knew vampires jump so HIGH?" Miles says in awe.

Suddenly, Sharptooth's face falls. She looks as though she's seen a ghost behind us (which we now know could actually be the case).

Following her eyeline, I swivel round. My blood goes cold. There, standing a few feet away, holding flashlights and staring at Sharptooth in horror are Mum, Dad, and Miles's parents.

They've seen everything.

"A vampire. An actual *vampire*."

Dad is pacing back and forth across our sitting room. Mum is sitting in the armchair to the side of the room, her hands wrapped around a steaming mug of tea. Every time she tries to sip it, her hands shake and it spills.

I close my eyes, slumping farther back into the sofa, wishing I could turn back time.

It turns out that Miles had missed soccer practice after school again, something that's happened a few times since Sharptooth came into our lives. At first, he managed to make an excuse that someone on his team passed on to the coach—something along the lines that he wasn't feeling well and had had to run home—and luckily it didn't get back to his parents. But then he stopped making excuses, too wrapped up in our adventures with Sharptooth to remember.

The coach was concerned, considering Miles is usually one of his best and most enthusiastic players, so he called his parents tonight to check in on him. They called my parents, found out where Miles was, and came to pick him up in order to ask why he was skipping soccer. He loves soccer, they thought.

When they couldn't get him on his phone and my parents couldn't get me—our phones were in our bags while we were talking to Sharptooth—they set out from the house to call us in.

You should have heard their screams.

I hope Sharptooth is OK. As soon as Miles's parents started screaming and running toward Miles to grab him and drag him away from the vampire, she disappeared into the darkness. She'll be back at the castle, worrying. I wish I could go see her.

At first we tried to tell our parents that they'd been seeing things, but it was no use. They'd arrived at the scene earlier than we realized and had witnessed Sharptooth's amazing vampire powers. Not to mention her ability to vanish into the night.

"A vampire," Dad repeats, still pacing manically and making me feel a bit dizzy, to be honest. "Right there, in front of our eyes."

"She came to our house," Mum reminds him, biting her lip. "She sat with us."

"And she didn't hurt you, remember? Or anyone," I say tiredly, having spent the last few minutes going on about how she was harmless. "I know it's a lot to take in, but—"

"There are vampires in the woods," Dad says, cutting me off. "They really do exist."

"Yes, they do."

"My God." Dad buries his head in his hands. "I can't believe it's really *true*. All of it."

"The myths and legends about Skeleton Woods? I know. It's crazy." I nod.

"Not just that, the other things that . . ." Dad trails off. Mum gives him a sharp look.

"What other things?" I ask, watching them curiously.

"Your dad just means the stories about Skeleton Woods," Mum says, waving her hand and brushing the question aside, before turning to me. "Maggie, how could you not *tell us* about all this?"

"You wouldn't have believed me," I answer truthfully.

"How long have you known about this vampire?"

"Her name is Sharptooth," I say firmly. "A few weeks."

"Weeks?" Dad stares at me from where he's leaning on the mantelpiece. "What were you THINKING? She's a VAMPIRE."

"But she's not a bad one! She's a vegetarian. She only drinks beet juice. She'd never hurt anyone. You've met her!"

His forehead furrows as he tries to make sense of what I'm saying. "Shar, yes. She was . . . polite. Strange, but polite."

"You see? She is a very well-mannered vampire. You have to tell the other parents. They need to know that she'd never hurt anyone."

"It's too late, Maggie," Mum says gently. "Miles's dad has already told Ari's parents. They'll be telling everyone else as we speak, I imagine."

"You have to stop them!"

"How can we? It's their right to do everything they can to keep their children safe." She closes her eyes in despair. "Their lovely, vulnerable children who have been spending time with a *vampire*."

"Ari and Miles are not vulnerable," I huff, jumping to my feet in anger. "We knew the risks and we didn't care. Sharptooth is kind, caring, and funny. She would never hurt anybody. I've told you, she's a vegetarian. She only eats beet juice and, now, ketchup."

"Is that why all our ketchup has gone missing? I wondered if . . . oh goodness!" Mum suddenly clasps a hand over her mouth. "That night she was here we cooked with so much *garlic*!"

"Yes, you did," I say, putting my hands on my hips. "Which goes to show how polite and lovely Sharptooth is. She put up with it. She simply ate her ketchup happily. And fainted every time she smelled the garlic."

Mum grimaces. "Oh dear."

"Look," I say, throwing up my hands in exasperation, "I

know that this is all ridiculous and surreal. I *know* that. I went through the same thing when I first met Sharptooth. But I'm telling you the truth, and you must know that, because you've *met* her. Dad, you shook hands with her."

He gulps. "Her fingers were like ice."

"She may be a vampire, but she's a good one. Please, help me persuade the other parents that she's harmless. And maybe then they'll keep her existence a secret."

"Your mum's right, Maggie," Dad says quietly, his eyes downcast. "We can't keep Sharptooth a secret."

"We have to!" I cry out, feeling like I might burst into tears, which never happens. "She's my friend! I have to protect her!"

Mum and Dad both snap their heads up to look at me.

"W-what did you just say?" Dad asks, peering at me in disbelief.

"I said, I have to *protect* her."

"Oh, Maggie," Mum whispers, her eyes glistening.

"What?" I look from one to the other. "What is it?"

"You weren't born to protect her," Dad says, staring me straight in the eye, his voice as serious as I've ever heard him. "You were born to kill her."

D ad comes down from the attic carrying a heavy, old book. He places it on the kitchen table, around which Mum and I are sitting, having waited together in silence for him to return from upstairs. He slides the book across to me and I read the title written across the cover in swirly gold ink.

How to Be a Vampire Slayer

I glance up at my parents. "What is this?"

"The house wasn't the only thing Uncle Bram left to us in his will," Dad says, taking a seat next to Mum and resting his elbows on the table. She puts a comforting hand over his as he explains. "He also left us this book. It seems to be some kind of . . . manual or diary. As far as I can tell, it has been added to by various family members over the years. And when I say years, I mean *years*. Some of the entries in there are very old."

I don't need Dad to tell me this book is old. It's practically falling apart. The cover is weather-beaten black leather, fraying slightly at the corners, and the paper inside has browned. Carefully opening it and flicking through the pages, I notice immediately that the handwriting changes several times throughout the book. Mum and Dad watch as I leaf through, examining the first few pages. There don't seem to be any names written in the book, so it's impossible to tell who each handwriting style belongs to. The starting pages look as though they were written on parchment using a quill and then somehow bound together to form the start of the book.

"This must go back . . . centuries!" I whisper, looking up at Dad. "How did Great-Uncle Bram have this? Where did he get it?"

"He explains in his letter."

"What letter?"

Dad glances quickly at Mum, who nods in encouragement. He pushes his chair away from the table, its legs scraping across the kitchen tiles, and then leaves the room.

I hear a drawer being slid out from his desk and then shut again before he reappears holding a crumpled envelope. He hands it to me before sitting down again.

I open the envelope and pull out the letter stuffed inside.

To the next Helsby Slayer,

This book has been passed down our family for generations. Guard it with your life. For in this book you will find all the information you need to keep the vampires of Skeleton Woods at bay, should they break their promise and attack Goreway.

As the story was told to me, so I write it here for you.

For centuries, the Helsby family has produced the best vampire hunters in the world—it is in our blood. When the vampire dynasty of Skeleton Woods made a home in the castle a long time ago, they did not know a Helsby lived at Skeleton Lodge. Afraid of the Helsby name, the vampires promised to only feast on the beasts of the forest and create enchantments around the woods so that the humans of Goreway would not stray toward the castle by accident, if it meant the vampires could live there in peace.

And the Helsby family made a promise to themselves

that there would always be a Helsby at Skeleton Lodge to protect Goreway and its residents, should the vampires get other ideas. There is no vampire enchantment that works on a true Helsby slayer.

If you are reading this, it is because you are the true Helsby slayer, descendant of vampire hunters throughout history. You must vow to protect the people of Goreway, just as I have done and those slayers before me.

The vampires may have made a promise a long time ago, but do not be fooled. You will see their bloodred eyes watching you from the woods. They are biding their time. Of that I am certain.

Read this book and learn from it. Protect the people of Goreway. You are the only one who can. It is your duty and your destiny. I pass this burden to you.

Good luck and remember, watch your neck.
Bram

I read it twice and then put it back in its envelope. "This is unbelievable."

"That's just the thing, Maggie. I read this and thought it

really was *unbelievable*," Dad emphasizes. "I'd heard the stories about Skeleton Woods and the vampires when I was growing up, and I have to admit that your mother and I, on reading this letter and receiving this book on Bram's death, did some research into the myths because it was all so strange, but I didn't really *believe* it. I thought it was nonsense! A silly family legend that Uncle Bram had become obsessed with, cutting himself off from the rest of the world in doing so. But now . . ."

He trails off, looking lost. Mum squeezes his hand.

"Now," she says, taking over, "we realize there must be some truth to it. The fact that we saw a vampire today, right there in front of us by the woods. There can be no doubt that vampires exist and do really live in the castle. Which means that . . . well, what Uncle Bram says in the letter and the book and everything, maybe that's all true, too."

"The enchantments bit definitely is," I admit, causing them to both stare at me in alarm. "It's a strange mist in the woods that makes humans run away, puts them in a trance. I've seen it. It worked on Ari and Miles, but . . ."

"But?" Dad prompts, wide-eyed.

"The enchantments didn't work on me."

Mum nods slowly. "Just like in Bram's letter. Helsby

slayers are immune to vampire enchantments. That's why they are the protectors."

"I feel like this is a dream," Dad says after a few moments of silence. "I'm going to wake up at any moment and everything will be back to normal."

I stare at Great-Uncle Bram's letter and the book resting on the table in front of me. Dad's right, it all seems too strange to be real, but things are starting to fall into place. All those questions I've had clouding my brain are starting to be answered. Things are beginning to make sense.

Like how the enchantments of the woods didn't work on me and how, according to the vampires, I don't have a smell. I'm starting to understand why I've always loved spooky things, why I'm naturally enraptured by the horror genre, and why I don't get nightmares. I get why I feel like I can sense Sharptooth before I see her, how I can spot those bright red eyes watching me a long time before she arrives. Suddenly, it makes sense why Sharptooth felt strange around Skeleton Lodge as opposed to anywhere else in Goreway, why something about the house made her feel unwelcome and uneasy.

Skeleton Lodge is where the vampire slayers live.

And I'm almost certain that I can now make a good guess about the mystery of the man who saved Arthur Quince. The Helsby who lived at Skeleton Lodge at the time stayed true to their word. When a Goreway resident was threatened, a Helsby protected them, reminding the vampire of their promise. The vampire was frightened because he was confronted by a true vampire slayer. Arthur Quince wasn't wrong after all.

"What are you going to do, Dad?" I ask finally, passing the book and the letter back across the table to him.

He frowns in confusion. "What do you mean?"

"Well, now that you know Great-Uncle Bram was telling the truth, what happens next? Are you going to meet with Sharptooth and make sure the promises still stand? I don't think she knows anything about any of this, but I reckon Count Bloodthirst does. He was probably the one watching Great-Uncle Bram from the woods. He's not the nicest of vampires, I've been told. You'll have to read through this big book, being the Helsby slayer."

Mum shares a look with Dad before clearing her throat and leaning forward, clasping her hands together.

"Maggie, I think it's clear that your dad *isn't* a Helsby slayer."

"What? But you just agreed that the letter all made sense! What more evidence do you need?"

"That's not what I'm saying," she continues firmly. "We believe this now. We've seen Sharptooth. But your dad isn't the one this book belongs to."

"I don't understand."

"Maggie," Dad says, deflated, "sometimes when I come into your room, you're looking out the window toward the woods. I can't believe I'm about to ask my daughter this question, but, by any chance, have you ever seen a pair of red eyes out there among the trees?"

"I . . . well, yes. I mean, I've seen Sharptooth's when we've met up, but the very first night we moved here, I saw them."

Dad looks crestfallen.

"What is it, Dad? What's going on?"

"Maggie, I'm not the true Helsby slayer. *You* are."

I wait for Mum to burst out laughing at Dad's statement, but she doesn't. She's staring right at me, just like he is.

"You're not being serious."

"Don't you see? I've never been drawn to the woods, Maggie. I've never seen the bloodred eyes lurking there, like Bram did. From the moment we moved here, something's changed about you. The history, the school, the house: everything about Goreway fascinated you, as though you were *supposed* to be here. You've been spending time with a vampire. A vampire! And not only are you unaffected and, might I say, still *alive*, but you've also prevented that vampire from attacking Goreway."

Dad hesitates, closing his eyes and breathing deeply.

"I may be wrong, Maggie," he continues, "and as much as I wish that it weren't so, it feels as though this book and letter were supposed to go to you on Bram's death, not to me."

As he slides the book back to me, I want to protest. I want to tell him he's wrong, because I'm nothing special. I've never been special. Why would this whole slayer-destiny thing skip a generation and land with *me*? I'm good at absolutely nothing. I'm as average as a person can be.

But . . .

Something clicks. It's as though I've known it all along. The connection I have with Sharptooth, how drawn I am to Skeleton Woods, how I never want to leave it behind, no matter how many vampires it holds.

I hadn't even noticed, but for the first time, I feel like I belong somewhere.

"Why would the Helsbys ever make peace with the

vampires?" I blurt out, a question that has been on my mind since I read the letter.

"So they wouldn't harm anyone in Goreway," Mum answers, watching me curiously.

"But the Helsbys are vampire *hunters*, right? So why would they just let them be?"

Dad looks to Mum, who shrugs, looking as thrown as he is. "What are you trying to say, Maggie?"

"I'm trying to say that I don't think the Helsby slayers were only that. Maybe they respected vampires, too," I say slowly.

"How is that *possible*?"

"Because somewhere in our family history, I think a Helsby met a vampire. And I think they liked them. Dad, we don't live here just to protect the residents of Goreway. We live here to protect the residents of Skeleton Castle, too!"

"Maggie . . ."

"I know that I'm right. We have to protect both sides from each other. You have to trust me. I know what I'm doing. It's like Bram said: It's my duty. But I don't think I can do this on my own. So . . ." I look at my stunned parents determinedly. "Will you help me?"

I can't sleep.

I spend so much time tossing and turning that eventually I give up and kneel up on my bed to look out the window, desperate to see a sign of Sharptooth. But there are no red eyes watching from the woods tonight.

Dad phoned Miles's parents and then Ari's, but neither of them picked up. He promised that first thing in the morning, we'll drive to their houses and speak to them. Both he and Mum are certain that they're likely in shock tonight, but by the morning may be a bit calmer.

I took the slayer book upstairs with me and read through some of it before my eyes got too tired to carry on. The entries I've read detail encounters with vampires and how the Helsby writing them got away with their lives. Some of the stories are pretty cool.

One of my ancestors discovered a vampire lurking in the

dark wings of a London theater, alerted after actors kept going missing mysteriously. Then there was the Helsby who stopped a vampire attacking Queen Victoria when she was doing a tour of the Midlands as a teenager—she was sworn to secrecy of the incident, but was so grateful to have survived that she declared to her Helsby protector that from that day forth she would keep a diary to remember that each day was a blessing. Another entry discusses the writer's dedication to finding a spot next to the stream that runs along the edge of Skeleton Woods in Goreway at which to sit while doing their research on the fascinating history of the town, simultaneously reminding any lurking vampires of their presence nearby.

I wonder if that was Mina Helsby.

I've hidden the book safely under my bed, with Great-Uncle Bram's letter tucked into the first page. I need to speak to Sharptooth. I have to tell her everything I've found out. But before that I need to make sure that her existence is kept as secret as possible.

I must eventually drift off to sleep in the early hours, because I wake up freezing cold from my kneeling position on top of the duvet, my head resting on my arms across the windowsill.

"Are you ready to go?" I ask Mum, coming into the kitchen showered and dressed, rubbing my neck.

She puts down her coffee, looking at me in alarm. "Have you hurt yourself? What's wrong with your neck?"

"It's not a vampire bite. I just slept funny," I assure her, attempting a joke.

"That's not what I . . . I didn't think . . . never mind." She shakes her head. "Sorry. This is all a bit overwhelming. For a moment this morning I wondered if I'd dreamed the whole thing. But your father tells me I didn't."

"It's going to be OK, Mum. You don't need to worry."

"Sure, of course," she says, throwing her hands up in the air and laughing manically. "I mean, what is there to worry about? My family has moved to a new house that's next door to a community of real-life *vampires* and I've discovered that my eleven-year-old daughter is destined to be a vampire slayer, but that's all completely normal."

This is a very typical reaction from my mum. Whenever she gets stressed, she gets very sarcastic. Sometimes it can be hard to tell what she means and what she doesn't, as Dad found out a couple of years ago when she replied, "Oh sure, absolutely, that makes sense!" to his question of whether he should knock through the kitchen wall to expand the space.

A couple of days later, she heard a loud crash and ran through to find Dad having a wonderful time swinging a hammer at the wall.

That wasn't a fun day for any of us.

"Maybe you shouldn't have any more coffee," I advise, calmly moving the mug away from her. "Mum, if you don't feel up to it, then you don't have to come with me today. I understand."

She sighs, leaning back on the kitchen counter. "I'll be right at your side, Maggie, no matter what. It's simply that . . . well, let's just say that I thought moving to the middle of nowhere from the busy city would be a calming experience."

"Nothing wrong with a little bit of adventure," Dad says, appearing in the kitchen and heading over to wrap his arms around Mum. "We always said we wanted that."

"Yes, but I didn't think it would mean stepping into one of the horror movies you two love," she points out, leaning her head on his shoulder. "Why couldn't it be a woodland full of charming fairies and pixies? Why couldn't the Helsbys be world-renowned fairy shoe cobblers or something?"

"Why would fairies need shoes?" Dad asks, confused.

"We should go," I jump in, tapping my watch before Mum can answer. "We have to get to Miles and Ari before their families tell someone who reacts badly to vampires."

"Someone who reacts badly to vampires?" Mum says dryly, picking up the car keys and heading toward the door. "What a CRAZY idea!"

Usually it takes no time at all to drive into town, but today there's chockablock traffic, everyone at a complete standstill.

"What is going on?" Dad asks impatiently as others beep their horns loudly.

"Something must be happening on the main street," Mum concludes, winding down the window to see if she can see anything farther down when she pokes her head out.

"It would be quicker to walk!" I say, exasperated. "Shall I get out and meet you at Miles's house?"

"No, we should all be together," Dad insists firmly. "Look, everyone is getting out of their cars and walking down. Should we do the same?"

"I don't think we have a choice. There's nowhere to turn

around," Mum says. "Come on, let's go. The car will be fine here with everyone else's."

I slide out and shut the door behind me, rushing to catch up with Mum and Dad as we join the crowd of impatient drivers marching toward the main street. The reason for the traffic jam becomes clear when we see that a temporary stage has been erected in the main square and the crowd of people surrounding it has spilled across the road, stopping cars from going either way.

"What is this?" Mum asks, craning her neck to see past the sea of heads in front of her. "Is it some kind of protest?"

"I'm not sure," Dad replies grumpily as someone bumps his shoulder to get past. "What are they chanting? And who is that on the stage? Oh! It's Mayor Cauliflower!"

As we finally get close enough to read the signs that the people up front are holding, my throat tightens and my stomach twists into knots of horror.

"Oh no!" I whisper, clutching Dad's arm. "We're too late!"

Homemade placards held above people's heads scream bold statements like RID GOREWAY OF VAMPIRES and PROTECT OUR FAMILIES! or TEAR DOWN SKELETON WOODS!

I shouldn't be surprised that word has gotten around so

quickly, but I'm shocked at how fast Mayor Collyfleur has moved to arrange this gathering. He stands up onstage with a microphone, nodding solemnly as his fired-up audience cries out about the dangers of Skeleton Woods, waving their fists in the air angrily. I ask Mum and Dad if either of them can see Miles and Ari anywhere, and the three of us desperately try to look for them somewhere in the crowd.

Mayor Collyfleur raises his hands for silence. Even from here I can see his beady eyes lit up with joy at the opportunity this has given him, and it makes my blood boil with rage.

"Residents of Goreway," he bellows into the microphone, his voice booming across the square, "by now you have all heard the news. Our town is under THREAT! Yes. I have heard the rumors. I have spoken to several EYEWITNESSES. Our town is under threat from those that haunt your nightmares. From VAMPIRES!"

The crowd gasps at his words, family members clutching one another in fear.

"I have to get to the stage," I say to my parents. "I need to tell everyone that none of this is true!"

Dad tries to clear the way ahead of us, attempting to move people so we can get closer to the front, but it's no use. Everyone is packed in together and no one listens to him. They're too busy listening to the mayor.

"A while ago I declared that the best thing to do for Goreway would be to tear down the woodland and build a golf course," Mayor Collyfleur continues gravely. "My plans were cruelly REJECTED by all of YOU!" He jabs his finger accusingly at the crowd. "But now you know that I was right all along! That I am brilliant! And that the only way we can protect our families is to BUILD A LUXURY GOLF COURSE AND CLUB THAT WILL HAVE A STATUE OF ME OUTSIDE IT!" He hesitates as people look to one another, slightly confused, before clearing his throat and continuing. "What I mean is . . . we shall TEAR DOWN SKELETON WOODS AND RID GOREWAY OF VAMPIRES!"

The crowd cheers and Mayor Collyfleur punches the air triumphantly.

"My dear Goreway residents," he croaks as the cheers subside, pretending to be moved to tears, but he's not fooling me, "we must stand together against this cruel enemy. We must fight side by side! And we shall win! I shall be leading a team this very afternoon to Skeleton Woods to chop down those trees. And for those who are worried among you, don't be." He grins menacingly, pointing his finger up at the sky where the sun is shining through the clouds. "Without their precious tree canopy, the vampires cannot last for long."

Concluding his rallying speech, he turns to his team lined up behind him on the stage to give them whispered instructions. The crowd's emotion erupts into a mixture of panicked frenzy and vicious determination.

Mum turns to me, worried. "Maggie, what shall we do?"

"I have to go find Sharptooth. I have to warn her!"

"I'm not sure that's a good idea. What if the vampires get angry when they find out they're under attack?" Dad asks, gripping my hand and squeezing it.

"Sharptooth wouldn't let any of them hurt me. And besides, they might just listen to her."

"Why would they listen to the one vegetarian vampire?"

"Because she's the Chosen Leader."

They blink at me, before Mum says slowly, "The Chosen *what*?"

"I'll explain another time. Will you take me to Skeleton Woods?"

"If you think it's the right thing to do, then I'm not sure

we have a choice." Dad sighs, reaching for the car keys in his pocket. "Although it feels like we're running toward danger."

"Trust me, Dad, we're not going toward danger," I say as we leave the square, glancing back at Mayor Collyfleur rubbing his hands with unashamed glee. "We're running away from it."

There are several things I would recommend that you do NOT do when strolling into a vampire castle, home to hundreds of vampires. This includes the following:

1. Probably best NOT to alert them all to your presence by catching your trousers on one of the nails sticking out of the front door and crying out loudly, "ARGH! My favorite JEANS!"

2. When you decide to hide just in case your spontaneous whining about your jeans alerted the vampires that you're there, find a GOOD place to hide.

3. Do NOT attempt to hide behind an old rickety table in the hall, on top of which are some lovely antique candle stands.

4. DO NOT THEN BUMP INTO the table, consequently KNOCKING OVER all the stands and their candles.

5. It helps if the table you bump into is not RIGHT NEXT TO an old flammable curtain.

6. It is NOT helpful to then yelp "FIRE!" at the top of your lungs when the curtain goes up in flames.

7. Best to keep a CALM, LEVEL head in these situations and not start running around, flapping your arms and shouting, "DOES ANYONE HAVE AN EXTINGUISHER?!"

8. When loads of vampires suddenly come along to see what's going on, the right action would be to RUN FOR YOUR LIFE, and NOT yell,

"CAN VAMPIRES PUT OUT FIRES WITH THEIR CLOAKS?!"

9. And when a vampire appears with a fire extinguisher and puts out the fire, it is sensible to then revisit point number eight on this list and RUN FOR YOUR LIFE.

10. Do NOT instead give the crowd of shocked vampires staring at you an awkward wave and say, "Phew! That was a close one! Lucky no one panicked, right?"

I'm not sure what I was expecting, but for some reason I'm genuinely startled to be confronted by a group of vampires and their bats in Skeleton Castle. I think I'd convinced myself that I'd be able to find Sharptooth before coming across any other vampire, and she'd be able to sort everything out for me.

Thanks to my clumsiness, however, I have not made the stealthy entrance I'd imagined.

"A *human*," one of the vampires whispers, watching me wide-eyed. "How did you get in?"

"I can't smell her!" another vampire comments, horrified, while his bat screeches in fear at his claim. "What's wrong with my vampire senses?! Is something wrong with me? Am I ill?"

"No, you're fine," I assure him, while my brain is busy going, WHY ARE YOU TALKING TO THIS VAMPIRE AS THOUGH HE IS YOUR PAL, HE IS PROBABLY ABOUT TO EAT YOU. "I don't have a smell. None of you can smell me, right?"

"All humans have a smell," another vampire says, narrowing her eyes at me and shuffling closer, which I do not care for.

Her bat sits on top of her head, baring his sharp little teeth at me. He is a lot more threatening than Bat-Ears, but I'll be sure never to tell him that.

"Well, I don't," I gulp, backing up slowly until I'm against the cold stone wall. "And that's because I'm a . . . I'm a Helsby."

"A Bellsby?" one vampire sniffs. "What's a Bellsby? Is it a type of bat?"

"She's obviously not a bat, Maggothead," another sneers. "She's a *human*."

"She said she was a Bellsby!" Maggothead retorts. "And

she doesn't smell. She doesn't smell tasty; she doesn't smell gross; she doesn't smell of anything. That means she could be a bat. They don't smell to us, either."

"That doesn't mean she's not HUMAN. Use your eyes, Maggothead."

"Use your nose, Dreadclaw!"

"You're being an IDIOT."

"You're being a BIGGER IDIOT."

"Sorry, I actually said *Helsby*," I correct them quietly, raising my hand before things get too heated. "It's my name. Maggie Helsby."

"Maggot-Helsby?!" Maggothead clasps a hand to his chest. "My name is MAGGOTHEAD! I can't share a name with a human! That's so EMBARRASSING!"

"MWAHAHAHA!" cackles Dreadclaw. "Maggothead is a STUPID HUMAN NAME!"

"That was the WORST cackle I've ever heard," Maggothead growls. "And if you dare—"

"Instead of arguing with one another," interrupts another vampire impatiently, "shouldn't we be, you know, attacking the human?"

"Good idea, Fangly."

Suddenly, all pairs of bloodred eyes in the hall swivel

hungrily toward me. I shudder at the sight, but then remember what I'd shoved into my pocket when Mum and Dad made a stop at the house before dropping me off at the edge of the woods. I quickly pull out a bulb of garlic and hold it above my head.

The vampires gasp and shuffle backward, furious at this turn of events.

"Look, I . . . I don't want to hurt you with these . . . uh . . . garlic cloves, but I will!" I croak, trying to sound a lot more confident than I feel. "I will peel each one if I have to and push it right up your nostrils! So stay back. Please. Thank you."

"Exactly WHAT is going on here?"

The voice that echoes off the walls chills me to the bone. Even the vampires jump at it, the circle they'd made around me parting quickly to let through the tall, sweeping figure that approaches. He stops suddenly at spotting the cause of the commotion.

This vampire needs no introduction. Count Bloodthirst is as terrifying as I'd imagined. His fangs are sharper and more protruding than the others', his mere presence is far more intimidating, and I'd recognize those eyes anywhere. They're the ones I saw the first night I arrived at Skeleton

Lodge. Redder, brighter, and with more evil lurking behind them than any of the others.

"*What is the meaning of this?*" he hisses, looking me up and down, his glance lingering on the bulb of garlic in my hand.

"She's a non-smelly human but also a bat, and her name is Maggot," says Maggothead, stepping forward to volunteer the information.

Count Bloodthirst sighs heavily. "Yet again, your stupidity astounds me, Maggothead."

Maggothead bows his head and trips over his cloak as he slides backward into the group. Dreadclaw looks delighted at this scolding.

"My name is Maggie Helsby," I announce clearly, looking Count Bloodthirst right in the eye, refusing to let him think I'm afraid.

"I know who you are," Count Bloodthirst replies bitterly. "The little girl from Skeleton Lodge. How did you get into my castle?"

"I walked. I actually caught my jeans on one of those nails on the door. That was inconvenient."

THAT WAS INCONVENIENT? I honestly don't know what is wrong with me, but for some reason I am talking to the vampire leader as though I'm having a pleasant chat with a stranger in a dentist's waiting room.

"I meant, how did you get through the enchantments?" he snarls.

"They don't work on me." I pause for dramatic effect. "I think you know why."

He starts, looking as though someone has just slapped him around the face. Then I see it flash across his face: *fear.* It's fleeting and he masks it quickly, but I've spotted it and it gives me the boost of confidence I need.

"So then . . . I was right when I first saw you," he whispers, the other vampires all watching him curiously. "You had the powers to see me. Not your father or mother. *You.*"

"Yep." I nod. "I'm the heir to the slayer . . . uh . . . qualities. If that makes sense. You know what I mean."

He narrows his eyes at me. "I see. Is that why you're here? To slay all of us?"

He gestures at the large group of vampires around him. They all begin to cackle. It's extremely unnerving that none of them smile while doing so.

"No, I'm not. I'm here to save you."

They fall into stunned silence.

"What did you say?" Count Bloodthirst asks in disbelief.

"I said I'm here to save you," I repeat, trying to sound confident in spite of the wavering in my voice. "You're in danger."

"Let me get this straight," Count Bloodthirst says slowly, "you, the successor of the famous Helsby slayer name, are here to save us vampires from danger? Sounds like a trap to me. But perhaps I'll let all the other vampires decide."

"I'm not afraid of any of you," I yell as a warning to the vampires edging forward, looking eager to make the decision as to whether I get to live or not. "If this was a trap, why would I risk walking in here on my own? You'd smell if anyone else was here with me, wouldn't you? The only reason I'm risking my life right now is to help you and your community. Ask Sharptooth if you don't believe me."

"*Sharptooth?*" Count Bloodthirst says in a strangled tone. "How can you POSSIBLY know who—"

"Maggie!"

At the sound of Sharptooth's voice, I feel a spark of hope. Relief floods through me as she pushes the other vampires out the way to appear at the front of the crowd, before moving to stand between me and them.

"What are you *doing* here, Maggie?" she cries, her expression thunderous. "You shouldn't—"

"I came to warn you, Sharptooth. The vampires are in danger. The mayor knows about you here in the woods and he's going to chop it all down so you have nowhere to go!"

She blinks at me. "Are . . . are you sure?"

"Yes. He's planning it as we speak, and he's coming here this afternoon. Everyone in Goreway knows about the vampire community here and they're scared."

Sharptooth looks crestfallen, her eyes falling to the floor. "Then we have to leave."

"Sharptooth!" Count Bloodthirst barks, prompting her to spin around and face him. "What is the meaning of this? What's going on?"

"Maggie is my *friend*."

There is a ripple of gasps at her statement and I hear the word *traitor* whispered.

"Vampires don't have friends," Count Bloodthirst seethes. "Especially not human ones. They are the enemy."

"No, they don't have to be," Sharptooth argues confidently. "If you could all just give humans a chance, you'd see that life is much better when you have a friend. I have three."

"Impossible!" Maggothead exclaims.

"It's not, it's fun! We listen to music and talk about human fiction books and catch Frisbees."

"What is this Frisbee you speak of?" Dreadclaw asks suspiciously. "Some kind of human disease?"

"No, it's a round thing," Sharptooth explains. "You throw it up into the air and catch it. Humans aren't very good at it, but I am brilliant at it."

"SILENCE!" Count Bloodthirst bellows, swishing his cloak back so violently it makes a cracking sound. "Sharptooth, do you realize who this is?"

He points his razor-sharp nail at me.

"Yes, my friend Maggie."

His eyes flicker to me. "You haven't told Sharptooth about your *family*, then, Maggie?"

"I only just found out myself," I reply hurriedly, hoping Sharptooth won't be angry. "And I swear, I'm not interested in hurting—"

"Maggie Helsby is a vampire slayer," Count Bloodthirst informs Sharptooth, enjoying every word. "Her family are destined to protect the humans from us. That's why the enchantments don't work on her and she is able to stroll in here whenever she pleases."

Sharptooth turns to look at me in surprise. "You're a slayer?"

"No! Well, yes, but no! It turns out all the Helsbys have this destiny to be vampire hunters. One is always living at Skeleton Lodge to protect the people of Goreway."

She gasps. "That's why I felt strange when I went there!"

"You *went* there," Count Bloodthirst seethes, his eyes flashing with fury.

"That's where I found ketchup," she tells him, putting her hands on her hips. "No regrets."

"Sharptooth," Count Bloodthirst says, his fists clenching, "your human acquaintance is the heir to the slayer name and has brought an army of humans to destroy our home!"

"No, that's not true!" I argue so fervently, he looks taken aback. "I would never want to destroy your home. I know this all sounds unbelievable, but Sharptooth and I really are friends. I respect her and I respect all of you. And I don't want our horrible mayor to destroy your home. I think, if we work together, we might be able to persuade the town of Goreway to leave you in peace. It's worked for me and Sharptooth, right? Think about it. If we could find a way to all get along . . ."

My sentence trails off. Count Bloodthirst is watching

me curiously, the other vampires all looking to him for instructions. Sharptooth takes a step forward, clearing her throat and lifting her chin defiantly.

"I'm the Chosen Leader," she reminds her fellow vampires. "My life is so much better with my human friends in it. I think we could change our ways and improve our happiness."

Count Bloodthirst shakes his head. "Vampires don't get to be happy."

"*Says who?*"

He stares at her. The vampires share confused glances and, for a moment, I feel a tingle of excitement run down my spine that they're even *considering* this.

Suddenly, they all turn their heads sharply to the left in unison, which, let me tell you, is VERY eerie. They must have all heard something, but I didn't hear a thing. It has to be far in the distance, unable to be picked up by human ears.

"What?" I ask, reaching out to tug on Sharptooth's cloak. "What is it? What's going on?"

"It sounds like machines," she says, her eyes widening with horror. "Loud machines. At the edge of the woodlands."

"It's the mayor! What about the enchantments? They'll keep them away, right?" I say desperately.

"The enchantments were created in harmony with the trees," Count Bloodthirst explains, his brow furrowed. "That was the doing of the Helsby family. It was you lot who wanted that as part of the deal, to make sure that the woodland would stay protected and neither the vampires nor the humans of Goreway would harm it."

"Can't you make some more enchantments now?"

"It's not vampire magic; we don't have that kind of power," he replies bitterly, disgusted at my lack of knowledge but at least talking to me as though I'm not the enemy anymore, which is something. "They were created with the help of the witches who used to live here. They moved out of the woods to integrate with the humans a long time ago. I could send a bat to ask a witch for help, but it would be too late by the time she gets here. The machines are creeping closer."

He turns his back on Sharptooth and me to address the terror-stricken vampires.

"The humans of Goreway have broken their promise, so we must now break ours," he announces. "Come! Let us prepare for battle!"

Led by Count Bloodthirst, the army of vampires glides along the stone floor of the castle toward the front door, their bats swarming above their heads, screeching and drowning out my desperate, helpless cries for them to stop.

18

Sharptooth looks at me in alarm, Bat-Ears flying in panicked circles round and round her head.

"What are we going to do?"

"I have no idea!" I reply, burying my head in my hands, my voice echoing around the now-silent hall of the castle, Sharptooth and I the only ones left behind. "This is a DISASTER. And it's all my fault! If I'd stayed away from Skeleton Woods like you told me to when we first met, none of this would have happened!"

"It's not your fault," Sharptooth says, stunned at my words. "Don't you think this was meant to happen? It was destiny! Just like in some of those human fiction books you gave me."

"I don't think I can pin this one on destiny, Sharptooth," I say, defeated. "Everything happening now is because of my careless decisions."

"But then, your decisions have brought about great change! Good change, I mean."

"What are you talking about? The vampire community that has been kept secret for all these years is now under attack! Because of me!"

Sharptooth looks at me as though I'm being stupid. "It wasn't kept secret. The humans always had a feeling we were here. We put up those enchantments, but it's not like we had loads of humans coming along to try them out. No one has been near the woods in years!"

"That's because of all the scary stories."

"Which were true." She shrugs. "So, like I said, you humans knew already, whether you wanted to believe it or not. The important thing is, you're here in the castle! Alive!"

"That's hardly an achievement. I've ruined everything."

"Maggie," she says, reaching forward to grip my hand in her ice-cold fingers, "that is a HUGE achievement. You persuaded Count Bloodthirst and all the other vampires not to attack you. They've just left! Knowing you're right here! Don't you see what that means?"

I shake my head, confused.

"It means we have *hope*!" she says, grinning at me, as

Bat-Ears finally comes to land on her shoulder, a little wobbly from all that circling. "We can still bring the two communities together. They liked you enough not to kill you. Why not the other humans, too?"

I stare at her. I guess what she's saying makes *some* kind of sense. They did let me talk long enough to argue my case. And they could have easily overpowered Sharptooth and me if they'd wanted to. Maybe something we said got through to them.

Maybe a teeny-tiny bit of Count Bloodthirst wants to be happy.

I mean, he likes bird-watching. You can't be THAT evil if you like bird-watching, right?

"OK, we *may* have more hope than I thought," I agree pensively, causing Sharptooth to straighten excitedly. "But how can we win both sides over?"

"I think we might already know the answer to that."

"You do?"

She nods cheerily. "FRISBEE!"

I blink at her. "Frisbee."

"Yes!"

"You want to try to stop an army of vampires and an army of humans battling each other by using a . . . Frisbee."

221

She gives me a sharp look. "Are you doing that human thing of speaking sarcastic? Because I read about that in one of the books, and your tone sounds very similar. Speaking sarcastic is very rude, Maggie Helsby."

"Sorry, Sharptooth, I don't mean to be rude," I say, unable to stop a smile at how cross she is. "It's just that I'm not sure a Frisbee is going to work. While it may be exciting to you, it's not that big a deal to humans. If we show up and wave a Frisbee around, they'd just think we were being weird."

"Yes, but what I mean is, that's why we're friends!"

"You've lost me."

She grabs my shoulders, the sudden coldness of her hands striking through my sweater and making me shiver. "If we can prove to the vampires that things like Frisbee and music and art and chatting are worth trusting humans for, then we can also prove to the humans that things like . . . uh . . . well, what do you like about me? Why haven't you driven a wooden stake through my heart?"

"Loads of reasons!"

"Then you can tell those reasons to the humans!"

She jerks her head up as she hears something.

"What? Tell me what you can hear."

"The machines have stopped," she says in despair. "I think because they've seen the vampires."

"Come on," I say, preparing for a swift exit as I gesture for her to grab me. "We don't have much time!"

"Mind if I just carry you? I didn't want to do that last time as it is quite scary for you, I'm guessing. But it is much quicker and then I won't break your legs."

"Sure. I trust you."

She steps forward and then throws me over her shoulder as though I weigh nothing at all, her cloak billowing behind us as we leave the castle. Suddenly, she bursts forward at the speed of light, and I have to shut my eyes, the ground is moving so fast beneath us. I've never had travel sickness before, but I sure do now.

She comes to a stop about two seconds after we've left the castle and props me down on the ground, already at the edge of the woods. I lean on her dizzily, my legs feeling wobbly beneath me.

"You all right?" she asks.

"I will be," I squeak, trying not to throw up. "I don't think humans are meant to go anywhere at that speed. Any chance you have any water?"

"There's the stream right there flowing around the trees,"

she points out happily, as though she's solved the problem. "I'll cup some of it in my hands for you to drink! You don't mind a bit of algae, do you?"

"Actually, I'm fine—thanks, Sharptooth," I say hurriedly, willing myself to feel better.

When my eyesight has come into focus and my legs don't feel as though they'll collapse at any moment, I take a look around to see what's going on. The vampires have spread out, careful to remain under the cover of the trees, but standing in a long line formation, staring out intimidatingly at the humans who have gathered at the edge.

Mayor Collyfleur is holding a megaphone at the front of the crowd and it looks as though he is currently instructing where his assistant should set up a small stepladder he's brought along, so that he can stand a few steps up from the ground and be higher than anyone else. The assistant obliges, helping the mayor to balance at the top. The crowd gathered with him looks frightened at all the red eyes staring out at them from the darkness.

"Who is that man?" Count Bloodthirst asks as Sharptooth and I rush to stand next to him in the center of the line of vampires. "The pompous one."

"That's Mayor Collyfleur," I tell him.

"Mayor Cauliflower, did you say?"

"Sure."

"Very well."

"Count Bloodthirst, please don't let your vampires hurt anyone."

"It's the humans who are attacking," he points out calmly, his bloodred eyes gleaming. "We're merely defending our home. Our promise to you, Helsby, will have to be broken."

"Let me speak to him first; I haven't had the chance," I plead desperately. "If he backs down, will you promise to?"

"I'm not making any more promises to any Helsbys," Count Bloodthirst huffs. "We've left the humans alone for years and lived only on the animals of the forest, and yet still they seek to destroy us."

"But most of them don't know that. If they knew you weren't going to eat them, maybe things would be different? To be fair, part of that is because of your . . . appetite. If you could work on that, then maybe things could be different."

He glances down at me, his forehead creased in

concentration. He doesn't trust me still, and I think he's trying to work out if this is all a trap.

"Fine," he says eventually, "go speak to Cauliflower."

"Thank you, Count Bloodthirst!"

I bow my head as I thank him, which I think is much appreciated as he looks very smug, and then I hurry from the woodland toward the mayor. People gasp and cry out as I approach, wondering how on earth I've come out of the woods alive. I notice they're all carrying garlic bulbs, some of them shoved into their pockets, others on string around their neck. A few of the angry-looking ones are even holding wooden stakes they've fashioned out of chair legs.

This has really gone much too medieval.

"Mayor Cauliflower—"

"COLLYFLEUR!" he bellows through the megaphone. "And don't come any closer! How do we know you're not a vampire?"

I stop where I am a few yards ahead of the crowd. "Because I'm standing in the sunshine? I go to Goreway School. I live at Skeleton Lodge."

"She might be a werewolf!" someone shouts out. "Or a witch!"

226

"As cool as that would be, sadly I'm neither," I reply, wondering if I should be complimented or insulted. "Just a normal, boring human."

"STAND ASIDE!" Mayor Collyfleur roars, his voice booming out the megaphone. "We're going to tear this woodland down and rid our town of those vampires!"

"We can see red eyes! A row of red flashing eyes!" his assistant cries, pointing a shaky finger at the woods. "They really do exist!"

"And we're not afraid of them," the mayor adds. "They're trying to intimidate us! But they shall not win!"

"Please!" I shout at the top of my lungs, holding up my hands. "They're not going to hurt you! They haven't all these years, have they? Let them live in the woods in peace!"

They all look stunned at my request, bothered by the idea that I might possibly be on the side of the vampires.

"You're just a CHILD!" Mayor Collyfleur smirks. "No one is going to listen to what you have to say! TEAR DOWN THE WOODS! GOODBYE, VAMPIRES! TEAR DOWN THE WOODS! GOODBYE, VAMPIRES!"

His chant catches on, and soon no one can possibly hear

what I'm trying to say. I wave my arms around madly, trying to regain their attention, but it's no use. Mayor Collyfleur chortles, stroking his chin triumphantly.

I've lost all hope when suddenly someone snatches the megaphone from the mayor's grip, causing him to stumble backward and almost topple off his little ladder. He looks thunderous at the culprit and their accomplice, two schoolchildren now racing toward me with the megaphone.

"Ari!" I beam at her and Miles as they reach me, both out of breath and grinning. "You're here!"

"Of course we are!" Ari says, passing me the megaphone and clapping me on the back. "We're not going to let our friends go it alone." She waves manically toward the woods. "Hi, Sharptooth! Not sure which of the pairs of red eyes looking at me you are, so just waving at all of you!"

We hear Bat-Ears's jubilant screech from the woods in response.

"Sorry we're late," Miles apologizes, rubbing his sweaty forehead. "It took us a while to persuade our parents to let us come and help Sharptooth."

"They feel really bad about starting all this." Ari

grimaces. "They shouldn't have sent out messages to the other parents, but once they told a couple of people, it snowballed."

"Don't worry, you're here and that's all that matters," I say, smiling at them in relief and tapping the megaphone. "And thanks for this."

"Use it well," Ari says, gesturing for me to speak. "We're here, ready to back you up."

I nervously hold it up, pressing the button on the top and immediately getting a horribly high-pitched squeak of feedback. Quite sweetly, the bats in the woods start screeching in reply.

"Uh . . . hello, everyone," I begin, jumping at how amplified my voice is, carrying across the fields through this thing. "I understand you may be scared of the vampires, but you don't need to be! They won't hurt you. My name is Maggie and I've been hanging out with a vampire for a while now. She's brilliant."

"She really is!" Ari says, leaning over my shoulder to add her voice to the cause.

"An amazing friend," Miles adds, too.

"We shouldn't be afraid of the vampires in Skeleton Woods," I continue, feeling much more confident now that

I have Ari and Miles next to me. "We should be *proud*. It's an incredible claim to have. Think about it! For centuries, vampires have been existing alongside the people of Goreway peacefully! Their diet consists of animals from the forest and that's it! And . . . and my vampire friend, Sharptooth, is vegetarian and lives off beet juice."

"AND KETCHUP!" a voice shouts out from the woods.

"And ketchup," I add with a smile. "Sharptooth is funny, smart, and kind. And I'm willing to bet that a lot of the vampires standing behind me are, too. The only reason they're here looking at you right now is because you're threatening to destroy their home. Why? For a stupid golf course that no one wants! It's my job to protect these woods and its residents, so I'm begging you all to reconsider. Please let them be. It's not just me asking you this, either."

I pass Ari the megaphone and nod encouragingly.

"Sharptooth is the coolest friend you could ever have," she says brightly. "She makes us laugh a lot and she's super enthusiastic about everything. She's getting very good at drawing, too." She hands the megaphone to Miles. "You tell them, Miles."

"Uh . . . the v-vampire we like, Sharptooth," he begins, tripping over his words, not a fan of public speaking, "well, she's nice. She doesn't judge you. Ever. She'll always be there for you. So that's important. And you should see her catch a Frisbee. I would show you now, but she'll turn to dust in the sun. So . . . yeah . . . it's amazing, though. Try to picture it. She's super fast and can jump so high. The point is . . . she's great."

"WE AGREE!"

My heart leaps at the sight of my parents, and Miles's and Ari's parents, all jostling through the crowd and running to come stand next to us, forming a small barrier between the mayor and the woods.

"What are you *doing* here?" Ari asks, hugging her mum.

"We believe you," Miles's dad says, the others nodding in agreement. "So we're here to support and fight alongside you."

Dad takes the megaphone and holds it up to his mouth. "Hello, Maggie's proud father here! Let me tell you that the vampire who came and had dinner at my house was extremely polite and well-mannered. I liked her a lot."

"Yes," Mum says, leaning in to announce her point. "We

served garlic bread and she was very kind about it. She didn't complain once, even though she was fainting every five seconds."

"Protect Skeleton Woods!" proclaims Ari's dad, punching the air.

Dad lowers the megaphone and we stand there together, watching the reaction. The crowd surrounding Mayor Collyfleur shuffles uncomfortably, talking to one another in hushed voices and shrugging.

"Look," Mum says, nodding to them, "they're changing their minds. It's working."

"TEAR DOWN THE WOODS!" Mayor Collyfleur bellows furiously.

"But why?" someone yells back. "If the vampires aren't going to hurt us, why should we destroy their home?"

"Exactly!" another agrees. "If they haven't harmed those children, what have any of us got to be afraid of? We should leave them alone."

"They're right, too. What about Goreway's heritage? Nowhere else has vampires in their woods!"

"Yes, it's our claim to fame!"

"Woodland should be protected. Think about its history! Not to mention the wildlife."

"START UP THE BULLDOZERS!" the mayor insists, stomping his foot on his stepladder and giving the drivers waiting a thumbs-up. But none of the engines start. Ari reaches over and squeezes my hand in excitement.

A woman standing near the stepladder folds her arms and looks up at the mayor. "Look, Mayor Cauliflower—"

"COLLYFLEUR!"

"The thing is," she continues, unfazed by his shouting in her face, "if we have the chance to protect and keep Skeleton Woods, then we should. And it looks like there's no reason to tear them down. Everyone agree?"

The crowd cheers and claps in response. Mayor Collyfleur looks as though he might explode.

"THIS IS NONSENSE! WE NEED TO TEAR DOWN THOSE WOODS!"

His assistant seems confused. "But *why*, Mr. Mayor? Everything is fine now."

"Everything is NOT FINE!" he spits, waving his fists in the air. "I NEED MY PRIVATE, LUXURY GOLF COURSE! I deserve it! I deserve it for all the hard work I do! I work every day from one p.m. until two p.m.! And this golf course is where I will be able to relax away from all of you lot!"

Everyone is shocked into silence, staring up at him as he prattles on, oblivious to his audience's reaction.

"I have earned this golf course!" he barks down at them. "Now do as I tell you and GO TEAR DOWN THAT WOODLAND!"

He finishes, placing his hands on his hips. The deafening silence in response would be unbearable if I wasn't so happy about it.

"Excuse me, Mr. Mayor"—his assistant bristles—"do you mean to say that this golf course isn't going to be open to everyone in Goreway? It's just going to be . . . *your* golf course?"

"Of course, you imbecile!" he hisses back. "What's the point of a PRIVATE, LUXURY golf course if it's not PRIVATE or LUXURY?! Now, I won't tell you again! Go get those vampires off *my land*!"

"I don't believe this," someone yells from the back. "You were going to use the tax money of your residents to build yourself a golf course that no one else was allowed to use!"

"And you were going to tear down our beautiful ancient woods!" another cries out.

"You used us, Mayor Cauliflower!"

"MY NAME IS COLLYFLEUR, YOU IDIOT! Why are you all such MORONS? I'll have my golf course," he roars, shaking his fist in the air, "or else! *Do you hear me?* OR ELSE!"

The crowd erupts into boos and hisses. The mayor begins to realize that he may have taken it too far, attempting to justify his actions.

"Now, wait a minute!" he says, stepping down from the ladder and trying to hide behind his assistant, who keeps stepping aside to leave him out in the open. "I'm the mayor! I can do what I like! You're not allowed to question my authority! It's my way or NO way! That's that! I deserve to—"

Suddenly, a bulb of garlic comes hurtling through the air and hits him on the head.

"HOW DARE YOU!" he shouts, angrily rubbing the spot where it landed. "If you must throw things, throw them at my assistant! Not at me!" Another garlic bulb splats against his arm. "Stop it! I'm the mayor! Stop it at once! I SAID STOP!"

As his assistant pelts a garlic bulb right at the mayor's chest, those surrounding him cheer his excellent aim, and suddenly there's a nonstop shower of garlic bulbs raining down on the mayor, who stumbles backward from the crowd and turns on his heel to run away.

"NO! LEAVE ME ALONE! NOOOOOOOO!"

He shrieks as the crowd chases him away from the woodland, pelting him with garlic bulbs. We watch him until he's just a dot on the horizon, disappearing from our view forever.

19

"WE DID IT!"

I burst out laughing at Ari's ear-piercing cheering through the megaphone as I'm enveloped in hugs from her and Miles. She's right. *We did it.* Together, we saved Skeleton Woods and, most importantly, Sharptooth.

Speaking of whom . . .

As Ari and Miles pull away to jump up and down in celebration, I look to the woods, the long line of red eyes waiting patiently for me to approach them. I interrupt Mum and Dad, both grinning and praising the other parents for taking a stand and saving an important piece of local history.

"I'm going to go have a word with the vampires," I announce, prompting them to all turn to glance nervously at the woods. "I won't be long."

"We'll wait right here," Mum says, pulling me in for a hug. "Proud of you."

"Shout if you need us," Dad says, ruffling my hair, before his forehead creases in concern. "And . . . well, don't get too close."

"Bit late for that, Dad," I laugh. "I was hanging out with them in their castle earlier."

He grimaces as I shove my hands in my pockets and walk off toward the line of trees. It's strange to think that I feel calmer as I approach the army of vampires than I did facing the mayor and his crowd of misled supporters.

When I think about it, that's how it's always been with me.

I guess it always will be.

"Well done, Maggie!" Sharptooth cries out, clapping her hands as I hop over the stream and step into the woods. "You did it!"

Bat-Ears launches himself from her shoulder and swoops into the air above me, somersaulting and screeching with joy. He hovers near me so I have the opportunity to tickle his belly before he returns to perch on Sharptooth's head.

"It was all your idea," I point out, beaming at her. "You were the one who told me what to do. In the end, I think it was the notion of how well you could catch a Frisbee that might have persuaded them you weren't all that bad."

She laughs and as she does, Maggothead yelps in horror and points at her face.

"What's *that*?" he asks, mystified, the other vampires equally as perplexed.

"I'm smiling," she tells him proudly. "I do that now. You should all give it a try."

"Let's not get ahead of ourselves." Count Bloodthirst clears his throat and glides toward me, his bat hanging upside down from the collar of his cloak. "Maggie Helsby, I'm . . . shocked."

"That I was telling the truth or that Sharptooth is smiling these days?"

"That a Helsby could be an ally." His brow furrows. "I almost feel bad that the day you arrived here, I planned on attacking you and your family."

"Oh!" I shift uncomfortably at this candid revelation. "Sure. I mean, you're a vampire. That makes sense, I guess."

"I'd always been taught to fear the Helsby name. I hoped that once that feisty Helsby gentleman who lived at Skeleton Lodge before you passed away, I might be able to . . . overpower his successor and expand the empire we have here in Skeleton Woods. But perhaps working together might just work. I must thank you for standing up to your fellow humans and protecting our home."

"You really have Sharptooth to thank for everything," I say, nudging her with my elbow. "She was the one who opened my eyes to how great vampires can be."

"All that's left for me to do is persuade you lot how great humans are!" Sharptooth declares to the vampires listening in. "But maybe that's unnecessary now, since you've witnessed it firsthand from Maggie here."

There's a ripple of murmuring agreements and excited chatter through the woods before we all fall silent at Count Bloodthirst raising his hands.

"Maggie Helsby, to thank you and your friends, I would like to invite you to a party at the castle next weekend. I can lower the enchantments that day so the other humans can make it through the woods. I think we'll be able to control our . . . urges."

"That's . . . *mildly* comforting," I croak, while Sharptooth whispers in my ear that she promises she will make sure everyone is safe and sound. "A party at Skeleton Castle sounds great. Thank you."

"I will send a bat to deliver the invitation with full details."

"You can send bats to deliver letters for you?"

"All the bats in the world are at my full command."

"That's AWESOME."

"Yes," he says slowly, his eyes narrowing as he studies me. "Maggie Helsby. Not much of a vampire slayer, are you?"

"Frankly," I sigh, smiling up at him, "I'm happy to say I'm a truly terrible one."

Over the next few days, something strange happens.

Everyone in Goreway begins to doubt what they saw. It happens gradually but surely. The rumor starts to spread that Ari and Miles and I made it all up. All those things we said about vampires and our "friend" Sharptooth. We did it, they say, to stop that greedy Mayor Cauliflower from destroying the woodland. It was, they tell us, *genius*.

Apparently, the mayor was the one who began the nonsense, claiming that he had heard that there really were vampires in Skeleton Woods. HA! Vampires? *Real* vampires? Don't be ridiculous! It was smart of him to play on the fears of those living in Goreway, to extort the myths and legends to fit his own agenda. How *embarrassing* that they all played along. That everyone fell for his little stunt in town, putting up that stage, rallying the crowd.

Goodness, what a lot of *drama*. And why wouldn't they get wrapped up in it all? There hasn't been anything interesting happening in Goreway for AGES! So, really, they shouldn't be ashamed of believing that horrible mayor (good riddance!), because, at the end of the day, it was rather a lot of fun! All for a good cause, too. How could they have thought for one moment that it would be a good idea to destroy the beauty and mystery of Skeleton Woods? Those woods keep Goreway on the map! Think of all the stories, the tales, the heritage that might have been wiped out with those bulldozers.

Of course, the children of Goreway School saved the day. It was such quick thinking to get all our friends to stand in a line in the woods holding a bunch of red lights that looked like pairs of eyes! How creative; really thinking outside the box there. Thank goodness the children of Goreway held fast to their principles, while all the adults lost their heads.

Skeleton Woods will be left alone for the rest of time and the people of Goreway will be sure of it. No one will *dare* to disturb them again.

"Amazing, isn't it?" Ari says, slumping back in her chair at the library table one lunch break. "How can they have shaken it off so quickly? They've convinced themselves in a matter of days! I don't understand."

"I think it makes sense," I say, reading the back of a new horror book that's just come in. "People believe what they want to believe. They always have. Look at Arthur Quince. He told everyone the truth. No one even bothered to at least go with him to see if it might be true."

"Yeah, I think you're going to have to give me a summary of Mr. Quince's story," Ari tells me, raising her eyebrows. "The chapter about him in that book you gave me is very long. Any chance you can tell me how it all turned out?"

"That's still a mystery. But if you want my opinion, I reckon he fled Goreway safely in search of a town with no vampires."

"Who would want to live somewhere like that?" Miles smiles slyly without looking up from the book he's reading. "To be honest, I think it's for the best that people think we've made it all up. Hopefully, the vampires will be left in peace. No one who fancies themselves a slayer to worry about."

I quickly look down at the book again, hoping they don't notice my cheeks flushing. I decided with Mum and Dad that it's probably best to keep the Helsby career tradition a secret.

"How are things with your soccer coach?" I ask, eager to change direction in the conversation. "All forgiven?"

"Sort of," Miles sighs. "I'm going to have to win back his trust, though, and make sure I'm on time for every practice from now on."

"We'll make sure we see Sharptooth around it." I nod firmly. "Now that our parents know about her, it's easier to tell them where we'll be and when."

Ari snorts. "Speak for yourself. My parents didn't see her, remember? They now think that Miles's parents and yours were in on this big ploy to save the woods. Dad keeps saying, 'Of course there are vampires in the woods,' and then doing a big dramatic wink at me or tapping the side of his nose. Honestly, I don't know how adults can be so stupid."

"I'm just glad Mayor Cauliflower is gone," I laugh, picking up another book from the stack of loaning options I brought over to the table and examining the cover. "At least I won't be evicted anytime soon."

The others nod in agreement. Mr. Frank emerges from one of the aisles pushing a trolley of books, and when he spots us, his expression lights up. He comes hurrying over.

"I hear you've all had an eventful few days," he says with a warm smile. "Well done for your brilliant work on saving the woodlands. Personally, I would have been devastated to lose them."

"I don't know what you're talking about," Ari says nonchalantly.

"Right, of course," he grins, winking at her and tapping the side of his nose.

She looks at Miles and me as if to say *You see?*, and we both have to hide our snickers.

"Ah, Maggie, you've hunted down the new horror fictions I've added to our collection," he says brightly, nodding to the uneven pile next to me. "Let me know if you'd like any recommendations. And I'll be eager to hear your thoughts on those." His eyes flicker to the book in Miles's hands. "I didn't realize you were a big horror fan, too, Miles."

"I didn't used to be," Miles admits with a sigh. "But thanks to recent events and Maggie's persistent recommendations, the genre is growing on me."

"Well, as I say, let me know if you need anything. And

thanks again," Mr. Frank adds, beaming down at us. "Perhaps you'll be inspired by these books, and one day, you'll write about your own great adventure saving Skeleton Woods and all the horrors it holds."

Suddenly, a bat comes swooping through an open window and lands with a dramatic thud on the table in front of us. The three of us jump and Mr. Frank screams at the top of his lungs, clutching a hand to his heart.

"WHAT THE—" He puts a hand over his mouth. "HOW did that get in here?! NOBODY PANIC!"

"It's all right, Mr. Frank," I say, jumping to my feet. "We'll keep an eye on it and maybe you can go get someone to help us capture it to set it free."

"Good idea!" he wheezes, starting to hyperventilate. "Back in a second! You . . . you don't panic or anything! Stay right there! REMAIN CALM!" He spins around and scarpers as fast as his legs can carry him out the doors, screaming, "BAT! BAT IN THE LIBRARY!"

We breathe a sigh of relief at his exit and, as Ari and Miles share a smile, I lean forward to address the bat.

"You can tell Count Bloodthirst that we got his kind invitation earlier this week and we haven't forgotten," I inform the bat, who tilts his head at me, listening carefully. "We'll be at the woods for six p.m."

The bat nods and then launches up in the air, flitting back out the window. I grin at Miles and Ari as I sit down, returning to my books.

"Our great adventure isn't over yet."

20

For the tenth time, Ari tells Miles to take off his scarf.

"It's rude," she hisses, trying to wrestle it off him as he slaps her away. "It makes it look as though you don't trust them."

"Firstly, it's not rude to wear a scarf when it's cold," he says crossly. "And secondly, I *don't* trust them! You think they won't be at all tempted by a nice juicy bit of neck floating around them?"

"Who says your neck is nice and juicy? It might be tough and gross."

"I'll have you know, Ari, that I moisturize my neck daily due to my sensitive skin."

"FINE. But you have to take it off when we're in the castle."

"It might be drafty in there," Miles huffs. "It's a very old castle."

"I've been sure to warm it up for you," a low voice says from the darkness.

They both jump as Count Bloodthirst appears beside them, his red eyes glinting playfully. I smile to myself, unsurprised at his presence. I had sensed him coming as soon as I led the way over the stream and into the very edge of the tree line, but hadn't wanted to interrupt the entertaining bickering of my friends.

"Good evening, Count Bloodthirst," Mum says, reaching out for a handshake.

Count Bloodthirst looks down soberly at her waiting hand, surprised at the confident gesture, before he takes it in his. She firmly shakes his hand.

I invited Mum and Dad to join us for the party tonight, because when I mentioned it to them, they honestly seemed eager to come. At first I thought it might be because they were being protective and didn't love the idea of letting my friends and me casually stroll into a castle full of peckish vampires without any chaperones, but, as well as that, I think they're very curious to learn a bit more about the Helsby world and heritage. Dad may not be a born vampire hunter, but he's always been the one to instill the love of the spooky in me. He wasn't about to let me have all the fun.

Mum was a little more hesitant about the party invitation, but now that we're here, she seems to be taking the lead. And, from Count Bloodthirst's slightly vulnerable expression after the handshake, I think he's understood that she's not the type to be messed with.

"Please do follow me," he says, swishing his cloak and leading us farther into the woods. "I shall be sure to walk at a snail's pace so your sluggish human legs can keep up."

"Wow, our host is a real joy," Ari mutters under her breath.

"I have lowered the enchantments for you," Count Bloodthirst continues, ignoring her. "But only for tonight."

"Smart thinking," I remark as we make our way to the castle, weaving through the trees. "One step at a time."

"Well, yes, that, and also, it's a nightmare to lower them," he admits with a heavy sigh. "I had to call in a favor with an old witch friend to help me out, and she wasn't very happy that I disturbed her evening. She was in the middle of a flying lesson with her daughter."

"I thought you said witches live among humans," Miles points out, tripping clumsily over a knotted branch and quickly regaining his balance before he falls flat on his face.

"They do."

"How can they have flying lessons, then? Surely, we'd notice witches flying about on their broomsticks."

"You'll be surprised to know what goes on right under your inadequate noses," Count Bloodthirst replies with a smirk. "Humans are notoriously ignorant. It's not that hard for witches to keep their broomstick flying lessons a secret, but, if necessary, they can always use an invisibility spell or use a warlock potion to wipe your memory should you see anything."

Miles gulps. "You're saying that we would never know if we'd seen a witch because they'd wipe our memory of it?"

"Worrying, isn't it?" Count Bloodthirst says breezily. "How much you don't know. Of course, if I'd known you'd be this interested in witches, I would have invited some to the party tonight. They're not big fans of vampires, but we've developed a sort of truce, so they might have been inclined to attend."

"That's all right," Miles insists, wrapping his scarf tighter. "A party of vampires is enough to be dealing with."

"Ah, here we are."

We reach the clearing and, finally, they all get to look up and admire the magnificent Skeleton Castle. I'm not sure

251

I've ever seen Dad so excited, his eyes filling with tears as he takes in the ruins.

"It looks just as I hoped it would," he says wistfully. "Exactly like in a horror film. You can picture Count Dracula here."

"Yes, there are many similarities to his abode," Count Bloodthirst informs us, gazing up at the bats fluttering about the crumbling turrets. "Although in my opinion, Dracula has a rather strange taste in candelabras, but that's neither here nor there."

Ari lets out a giggle. "You're making it sound as though Dracula is real."

Count Bloodthirst stares at her. She stops laughing.

"Is Count Dracula r-real?" she stutters, her eyes widening.

"If you would all like to come this way," he replies without answering her question, leaving her to stare after him open-mouthed as he opens the door to the castle.

We're led into a noisy, candlelit ballroom where the vampires have all gathered, ready to greet us. They fall into a hushed silence of anticipation as we traipse in nervously.

There are two long tables at each side of the room. On one table, a sign in messy handwriting reads STUFF FOR

THE HUMANS, and on the other side of the room, the sign on that table announces it's STUFF FOR US VAMPIRES. On the human table, there are vast platters of nibbles carefully laid out, alongside bottles of any drink you've ever heard of. I've never seen so many different colors of soda in my life.

Over on the vampire table are just rows and rows of beet juice cartons and ketchup bottles.

"You're here!" Sharptooth comes bursting through the doors and in a flash is at my side, gesturing to the human food table. "What do you think? Did we do it right?"

"It's BRILLIANT!" I exclaim, with vigorous nods from my fellow human guests. "What an incredible spread. I've never seen anything like it. Thank you so much!"

"Maggothead and Nightmare were in charge of the drinks"—they both give us a modest wave from the other side of the room—"and Dreadclaw helped me in the supermarket with all the food."

"You went to the supermarket?" Mum asks in amazement. "How?"

"Oooh, it was so fun," Dreadclaw enthuses, coming over to tell us all about it. "We researched which one was open at nighttime and then we went in DISGUISE."

"That's so cool! What disguise did you wear?" Miles asks.

"We wore *sunglasses*."

Everyone waits for Dreadclaw to continue, but that seems to be it. He looks at us, eager for our reaction.

"You . . . you wore sunglasses? That was it? That's how you got away with going to the supermarket at night?" Miles confirms. Dreadclaw nods excitedly. "Well, that's . . . great! Really good disguise."

"Thanks. The man at the till asked me if we were in a rock band and I said no, we were in the supermarket," Dreadclaw informs us. "Humans are so stupid! It was thrilling."

"It sounds like you had a blast," I chuckle. "Thanks to all of you for this."

"Welcome to Skeleton Castle, our new *friends*," Count Bloodthirst announces, his voice bouncing off the walls. "As you humans say, let's get this party started!"

Sharptooth signals at a vampire in the corner of the room, who is sitting on a large speaker and holding the end of a wire in one hand and a phone in the other. At Sharptooth's wave, she cautiously plugs the wire into the phone and jabs her finger at the screen. Music booms out of the speakers and she gets such a fright, she topples over backward.

The vampires erupt into cheers and, without hesitation, throw themselves around the dance floor, bopping around and waving their limbs about wildly without a touch of inhibition, dancing as though they've never danced before.

Which, now that I think about it, I guess they haven't.

Count Bloodthirst invites Mum and Dad to dig into the canapés, asking them whether they'd consider giving the vampire community a good deal on dental care, before launching into an enthusiastic conversation about the birds to be found in Skeleton Woods, offering to lend them his notes should they ever be interested in the species he's seen over the decades. Maggothead bops over to Ari and Miles, persuading them into the middle of the dance floor, where they eventually decide that the vampire style of dancing is way more fun than their usual, more cautious moves.

Sharptooth and I stand at the back, content to observe the wonderful chaos unfolding in front of us.

"Count Bloodthirst called me in for a serious chat in his office the other day," she tells me. "He wanted to tell me the truth about how I became a vampire and the whole Chosen Leader thing."

I frown at her. "What do you mean the *truth*?"

"The prophecy told him all those years ago that the next Chosen Leader of the vampires was a little orphan girl," she says, staring straight ahead. "But when he arrived at the orphanage where she was, something happened. He was just about to turn her into a vampire when another human orphan jumped in front of the other girl to save her. Apparently, this orphan didn't hesitate to tell Count Blood-thirst that he was evil and wrong to hurt anyone, and that if he wanted to hurt that other girl, he'd have to go through her."

She pauses, her eyes falling to the floor before continuing with the story.

"He was so astounded by this little girl's bravery and determination to protect others that he decided she should be the Chosen Leader instead. He thought she would be a great leader who would protect the vampire community. Apparently, at the time, he'd been having some doubts about his . . . evil way of life. In that moment, he decided that this child might be the one to change things one day. He thought that she'd be able to make vampires finally *happy*."

She smiles up at me. I don't know what to say, so I just stare at her, a dopey grin on my face, hot tears pricking at my eyes.

"In his office, he told me that recently he'd forgotten why he chose me in the first place," she discloses. "He said that he'd unwittingly turned into the leader he never wanted to be. But my friendship with you had reminded him what things could be like if we made some changes. He said that although he didn't listen to the prophecy when it came to picking the Chosen Leader, it was the best decision he'd ever made."

"Sharptooth," I manage to whisper, blinking back the tears as she finishes, "that's amazing."

"I feel like everything finally makes sense," she sighs, watching Count Bloodthirst over by the human table busy enacting the motions of a woodpecker, to the delight of my parents. "I just hope that I live up to it all."

"Of course you will," I assure her. "And if you need any proof of the positive impact you've already made, I want to show you this."

I reach into my bag and pull out the most important item I'd been sure to bring along to the party. It's a beautiful leather-bound book that Dad bought me this week as a special gift. He'd had a personalized inscription etched across the front in gold, swirly lettering:

How NOT to Be a Vampire Slayer

"It's the *new* Helsby manual to be handed down the generations for whoever lives in Skeleton Lodge. If you ask me, the old one was a little out of date," I explain as she admires it. "I'm going to write down how we met and detail all our interactions, along with any tips we can offer each other, so future Helsbys know the best way to keep the vampire community safe and happy. You see, Sharptooth Shadow? You've already changed things for the better a lot more than you know."

We both look out at the ballroom. Count Bloodthirst, Mum, Dad, Ari, and Miles are now all in the middle of it, dancing away with the vampires and having the time of their lives. Miles unwinds his scarf to great applause and lobs it to Maggothead, who uses it to start a limbo competition with Ari and Dreadclaw.

"Who would have thought it?" I say eventually, feeling so happy I might just burst.

Sharptooth turns to grin at me, her fangs glinting in the disco lights.

ACKNOWLEDGMENTS

Thank you to Yas, Lauren, Ruth, Pete, and the talented team at Scholastic. I feel so lucky to work with you all and I am forever grateful to you for bringing Maggie and Sharptooth's story to life.

To my absurdly wonderful agent, Lauren, thank you for everything you do. Twenty books together, can you believe it? Here's to the adventures to come.

Huge thanks to my family and friends. You provide never-ending inspiration with your wit, wisdom, and kindness. This book is dedicated to Mags, who brought fun and laughter to everything, with great style and a cracking sense of humor. She is very much missed.

Special thanks to my canine companions, in particular my little rescue dog, Bono, whose magnificent ears inspired Sharptooth's sidekick, Bat-Ears.

And to my readers, I really can't thank you enough for your support. As ever, I very much hope that this book brings joy and makes you smile.

ABOUT THE AUTHOR

Katy Birchall is the author of *How Not To Be a Vampire Slayer*, the Morgan Charmley: Teen Witch books, The It Girl series, and the Hotel Royale series. A lifelong fan of bonnets and trailblazing female authors, Katy was proud to create a retelling of Jane Austen's *Emma* for the Awesomely Austen series, a collection of Austen's novels retold for younger readers. When she's not busy dreaming up new characters, Katy also works as a freelance journalist and has written a nonfiction book, *How to Be a Princess: Real-Life Fairy Tales for Modern Heroines*. Katy lives in London with her husband, Ben, and her rescue dog, Bono. You can find her online at katybirchallauthor.com.